THE BALLAD OF
DANI AND ELI

Other books by Nicholas Bruner
Jesus Bugs
The Love Machine
Roll dem Bones

All books available at Amazon
(amazon.com/author/nicholasbruner)

Sign up for my mailing list and receive a free short story! **nicholasbruner.com/contact**

THE BALLAD OF
DANI AND ELI

The Ballad of Dani and Eli
© 2020 Nicholas Bruner

ISBN 978-1-970071-06-1

Cover design by MiblArt
Book design by John H. Matthews

Published by Bluebullseye Press

This book is dedicated to Billy Joe.

PART ONE: SUMMERTIME

CHAPTER ONE

The great old she-bear rose on two legs and sniffed the air. Moisture, a bit of charge in the atmosphere, meant a storm coming. But something else too. A scent that made her stop, stirred a memory, brought images of a connection. Perfumed, covered up as they do, but unmistakable: human sweat. A car came speeding around the curve on the road below the hillside where she perched, confirming her intuition. The teenage girl sat in the backseat, looking out the window. Yes, the she-bear thought. This is the one she had been waiting for.

I shoved my suitcase in the corner and laid the guitar case on the bed. I unlatched it and removed the Alvarez AD80SSB acoustic guitar. Rosewood with a sunburst finish. I caressed the neck, inspected the body for damage.

Not a blemish, thank God. Someday I'm going to play that beautiful thing in front of thousands. Until then I just have to keep practicing.

I strummed a chord. Out of tune, no surprise after the hot ride all day in the car trunk. I took a few minutes to tune it. A few quick scale exercises, to keep my fingers limber, and then I set it gently back in its case and headed out.

"Hey, Dad, I'm going for a walk," I called as I opened the screen door.

"Good idea, Dani, take a look around," came his voice from where he was unpacking in his bedroom. "How long will you be?"

"I don't know. Forty-five minutes, maybe?"

"Make it half an hour, we have to be at Aunt Eunice's at six."

The screen door slammed behind me and I hopped down the steps. The rental house was gray clapboard, a scraggly dogwood out front, driveway just a bare spot in the lawn. A couple other rundown houses sat across the street, which didn't look like it'd ever been repaved. Down a short hill the street ended in a T-intersection at the two-lane road the locals call a highway. A farming equipment store occupied one corner of the intersection, a gas station with a dinosaur on the sign the other.

Ryan whooped like a crazy person from somewhere in the trees behind the house, probably shooting zombies or something. He's eight years old and some days I think I might kill him before he gets to nine. I could tell it wouldn't be long until he went native here. I didn't plan to let the same thing happen to me. I put in my ear buds and let the music soothe my frazzled brain while I walked: Janis Joplin's *Pearl*, the best album ever recorded.

A quarter-mile down the highway I reached the parking lot of the Piggly Wiggly. A huge sign in the front window informed the world Mrs. Mac's fried chicken was on sale in the deli. Next door were a furniture store and a pizza joint. There didn't seem to be much action there so I kept walking. A little farther on I came to a row of stone buildings lining the road. The old downtown. There were actually some cool stores here. A music store with stringed instruments I didn't recognize in the window. An antique shop. Something called the Adelaide Cultural Center.

I stopped in front of it. Wooden steps led up to the entrance. The place was closed but I stepped up to read a poster hanging on the door. *Adelaide Music and Cultural Festival. August 14th-17th*. There followed a long list of bands and musicians who would be playing. I skimmed a few of the names. *The Mountain Home Boys. The Copeland Family. The Grave Mountain Singers. The Gin Soaked Boys.* I blinked and made sure I'd read that last one right.

A white pickup truck drove up the street while I read, slowing down as it neared me but not stopping. Oh, God, this town was so tiny the inhabitants checked out strangers. How was I going to make it here a whole summer? Lots of time to practice the guitar, at least.

It'd been about fifteen minutes so I pulled the poster down, rolled it up, and headed back. The white pickup had stopped in the parking lot of the Piggly Wiggly, its engine idling noisily. The truck was dirty and the letters on the tailgate read "C-H-V-Y." I knew whoever was driving it was waiting for me because there were about a thousand empty spaces closer to the store he could have parked in. The window rolled down as I approached. I pulled out my ear buds and dug my hands in my pockets. The driver looked me over like a piece of produce.

He was maybe seventeen, short dark hair, wore a jean jacket over a white tee. But oh man his brown eyes, big and vulnerable, like a deer startled in the woods. "You're new around here." Wasn't a question. One side of his mouth lifted in a crooked half smile. "You need a lift somewhere?"

"No, thank you. I'm just going behind that gas station." I nodded toward the dinosaur sign.

"Oh, so you the one renting the old McCollum place back there. You and your brother and your daddy, right?"

News got around fast here. "Um, yeah. That's right."

"Name's Austin." He reached his hand out. "Austin Campbell." I stepped up to the window and shook it. His grip was a little stronger than I was used to, his hand calloused.

He stared at me for several seconds and didn't let go. I felt a little nervous because he wasn't saying anything else. Was I going to have to stand in the parking lot holding his hand all night? "So, what's your name?" he finally asked.

Oh, that's why he wasn't letting go. Why was I so cool in situations like this? "Dani. Dani Moser."

He relaxed his grip and I put my hand back in my pocket. "Dani Moser," he repeated. "I saw you checking out the Cultural Center. You like music?"

"Definitely. But not country music so much."

Austin laughed, and I realized I'd said something stupid. "Country music's from Nashville," he said. "What we play here is something we call old-time. Or traditional. You might call it bluegrass. You interested in goin'?"

"Sure."

"All right, we'll go Friday night," Austin said. He started to roll up the window. Had I just arranged a date?

"Wait. What time will you pick me up?"

Austin laughed again. I liked the way it sounded. "Well, normally folks just meet in the parking lot of the Pig whenever."

"The Pig?"

"The Piggly Wiggly. Since you're new here, I guess I can walk you over. How 'bout eight?"

"Eight. Right. Sounds good."

"I'll be seein' you, Dani." He shifted into gear and his pickup truck rolled off with a roar and a cloud of smoke. Well, the locals were friendly, at least one of them. And Austin was pretty cute. Maybe things were looking up.

Aunt Eunice's big A-frame house was situated on the side of a mountain that's ten miles from anywhere, even what passes for anywhere in those parts. She called the house Springbloom, and it was like an overstuffed museum packed with leather-bound books, National Geographics, garden tools, China dolls, trunks of old clothes, newspapers from the second World War, musical instruments from India, vegetable seeds, lost keys, buffalo skulls, and practically anything else you would never think to imagine. I swear every time I go there I find a room I've never seen before.

Even before entering the house, Ruskin bounded out to greet us. Ruskin was Aunt Eunice's Irish terrier, and practically owned the house. We walked through the screen door into the kitchen, which was right in the front because it's the most important room in the house, the heady smells of chopped parsley and frying onions filling our noses. It was exactly the way I remembered it. Bundles of dried plants and copper pots hung from the ceiling, bookcases filled with cookbooks and jam jars lined the walls, fruits and mushrooms and herbs sat piled in unmatched bowls on the island. The sink was overflowing with dishes and the oven on, just like always. Aunt Eunice looked up from a cutting board when she heard the door open.

"Oh my, Dani!" She dropped her paring knife and hurried to embrace me. I breathed in her scent, a mix of pipe tobacco and baking spices. Her gray hair was braided down her back, a bird feather stuck behind one ear. "My Lord, you're a young woman now. How long has it been, do you think, since I saw you last?"

"Four years, Aunt Eunice." But it didn't matter,

she was already on to Ryan.

"And the last time I saw you, Ryan, you were just a little boy, walking underneath the dining table between our legs at Thanksgiving! Look at you so grown up!" The instant she released him, my brother grunted something about a zombie infestation and shot off into the house. She didn't seem to notice.

"How are you, Aunt Eunice?" my father asked her as she hugged him in turn.

"Better than ever, Jim. Sixty-one is the best year of my life. I know you don't believe me but you'll see when you get to my age. Now, don't let me forget I've got an applesauce cake baking for you. Your favorite, when you were a boy."

"Still is." He grinned broadly, and for a second the worry creases in his forehead disappeared, his eyes lit up, and he looked the way he did when I was little. "I can't believe you remembered from so long ago."

"Jim, I couldn't forget your favorite dessert if I tried. Although I do think you've lost some weight." She gave my father's belly an accusatory pat. "I suppose the situation with Deborah is affecting your appetite." Aunt Eunice was not a big believer in mincing words.

Before Dad could answer, Ryan bounded back in the room with Ruskin a step behind him. The dog caught up to Ryan and started licking his hands.

"Ruskin, stop that!" Aunt Eunice said. She pointed a finger at Ryan. "You must have been eating something and not washed your hands. You'd think I never fed this dog."

"Aunt Eunice, can I take Ruskin on a walk?" Ryan asked.

"Of course, dear. But let me give you some lettuce to drop off at the turtle pen. Ruskin'll show you where to go, you just follow him." She kept talking while she rummaged through the refrigerator. "Last week I found the first turtle I've seen this year and brought him back.He was trying to cross that new highway near Batestown. Can you imagine how he wasn't smashed with all those big trucks whizzing by there?"

She handed him the lettuce and my brother and Ruskin were gone with a slam of the screen door. "Now, Dani," she said, looking me up and down. "Tonight we certainly must talk. You're getting to the age when young people have interesting things to say. I hope you're not one of those who only has an interest in boys, are you?"

I smiled a little self-consciously. "I don't think so. Maybe a little bit."

"Well, we'll find out after dinner. Now, do something for me, if you would. Take this scissors and go cut some parsley in the back garden. You know what parsley looks like, right dear? And while you're back there, get some chicken breasts for me out of the deep freezer. Four should be enough. But take care when you open the freezer door, I have a rattlesnake frozen in there."

It took a moment for that to sink in but she'd already started chatting again with Dad before I could ask her about it. Apparently having a poisonous snake next to your Lean Cuisines is no big deal to Aunt Eunice. I set out to the back of the house with more than a little trepidation. I could practically hear the thing hissing as I approached.

It struck me: I was 700 miles from home in Minneapolis. Marooned in Adelaide, Arkansas, the middle of nowhere, the most isolated place you could imagine, until school started again. Two-and-a-half months without friends, television, restaurants, Mom, or civilization. So remote the only place we could seem to get cell service was our rental house. And after only an hour in town, I realized I might not even survive opening the deep freezer behind my Aunt Eunice's house.

CHAPTER TWO

"Mom, I am so ready to come home now," I said into the phone, huddling under the faded quilt covering my bed. The ancient rattling window air conditioner in my room had two settings: off and Antarctic. I'd sweated off about two pounds earlier and so was currently opting for Antarctic. Maybe Dad would let me adopt some penguins at some point.

"Dani, you've been there three days. I hardly think you've given it a chance." I could hear her tapping away on her keyboard in the background. "I bet hearing about the will must have been interesting."

"Going to the lawyer's office was the most boring mistake of my life," I said, pulling a corner of the quilt over my exposed foot, which was in danger of frostbite. "Besides, dealing with that stuff puts Dad in a bad mood."

"I'm sorry to hear that," Mom said, sounding a little exasperated. Mom is a corporate lawyer with a big law firm in Minneapolis. She's a very busy person and not very patient when you call her at work, where she always is. Dad, on the other hand, has all the time in the world since he lost his job. "Maybe you should try spending some time with your brother."

"If I go to the Pig with Ryan to get a snack one more time his hyperactivity might actually drive me to the brink of insanity."

"The pig?" she said. "Now that's something new. How often would you get to go to a farm up here?"

"No, Mom, it's just a grocery store."

I could hear somebody saying something to Mom about a meeting on the other end of the line. "Well, give the place some more time. I've got to go now. We'll talk longer next time, okay? Bye, dear."

"Bye, Mom," I said, sighing. Other than the law office and the Pig, I'd basically done nothing else but practice guitar and listen to Janis, fantasizing about playing on stage at the 1967 Monterey Music Festival, just like her. Dinner was over and I had nothing to look forward to for the rest of the evening but watching Dad solve a crossword and Ryan pick his nose. So, the surprise knock at the door couldn't have come as more of a relief.

"Dani, it's someone here for you!" Ryan bellowed as if I were in a far wing of our mansion, rather than the next room over in our tiny rental house. I put down the phone and went up front.

"Hey, Dani." It was Austin, looking through the screen. He had his hands in his jeans pockets and wore a plain black t-shirt. And he still wore those killer brown eyes.

"Oh, hey Austin. But it's not Friday yet."

"Nah. But I have to go to church tonight. I thought maybe you'd want to come."

"Tonight?"

"Yeah. Wednesday night, you know."

"Oh, yeah," I said. But I didn't really. Wasn't church supposed to be on Sundays? Whatever, anything to get out of the house. "Um, sure. Let me just change clothes." I went back to my room and tore garments out of my dresser. "Dad, I'm going to church with Austin!" I yelled out. Church. Did that mean I had to dress up?

"What? Who's Austin?" he yelled back.

"That guy I was telling you about! C'mon, Dad!" I found a nice white blouse. Good enough, hopefully. I decided to leave on my jeans. A few seconds to put on lipstick and voilà.

As I passed through Dad looked up from the

kitchen table where he was hunched over a week-old *New York Times* with a ballpoint pen. "Okay, honey, don't be too late."

"We shouldn't be more'n a couple hours, Mr. Moser," Austin said from the porch where Ryan was now shoving his handheld game machine in Austin's face and running on at the mouth.

"...and if you use the sword you can cut that guy right in half, and you can see his spine sticking out right there, cool right? But you don't know he's dead for sure unless you cut off his head or burn him..."

I stepped out and pushed my brother aside. "Oh, God, I'm so sorry to subject you to that."

"It's cool," Austin said. "I've never seen that game before."

"Hey, come back sometime and I'll let you have a turn," Ryan called after us as we stepped into the yard.

Austin waved to him. His white Chevy truck was parked in the street, still running. He opened the door for me and I climbed in.

The church stood in a field outside Adelaide. It looked like an old warehouse or something, with metal siding and no windows, cars parked outside on patchy grass. A signboard out front read "Nazareth Free Church: This Church is Prayer-Conditioned."

Austin and I walked in together. I was surprised to see the place packed. Not just old folks either, but teens there with their parents, little kids. There was a stage set up at the front with drums, a keyboard, a couple acoustic guitars, a guy tuning a bass. People were dressed casually.

A middle-aged man with a big belly approached us, the top two buttons of his French blue dress shirt unbuttoned and his sleeves rolled up. "You must be Dani," he said, putting out a beefy hand. I took it. "I'm so sorry about your granddaddy. We were all real fond of Doc Moser."

"Does everybody in town already know who I am?" I asked him.

His chubby face fell for a moment at my comment but then perked back up. "Well now, that was rude of me, wasn't it? Not even introducin' myself. I'm the preacher of this house of God, but we don't stand on ceremony here. Everyone just calls me Joab. I am so glad you could make it tonight. Now while you're staying here in town, you let me know if you need anything and I will be most happy to oblige."

"Sure," I said. "I guess." His offer seemed over-generous since we'd just met. A little creepy, even. I chalked him up as insincere.

He turned his attention to my companion. "And how are you gettin' along, Austin?"

"Fine, sir." Austin's voice had a slight edge. Was there something about Joab he knew?

"You finished cleaning that shed out yet?"

"I couldn't 'cause I had to eat supper." He looked at the ground.

"All right now, you finish up first thing tomorrow mornin'."

"Yes, sir."

Another group of parishioners entered the church and Joab turned to greet them with a hearty backslap. I leaned over to Austin and whispered. "You work for Preacher Joab?"

Austin smiled but kept those brown eyes cast down. "I guess you could say that. He's my daddy."

While I was processing that, the musicians got under way at the front of the church. The song wasn't one I was familiar with, a lot of Praises to the Son and Hallelujahs. Everybody else knew the words, though, and the musicians were good. The music's energy soon had people raising their hands, the drummer and bass player laying down a groove, the guitarists strumming and singing. Joab was up there too, banging a tambourine against his thick thigh and singing with his eyes closed. By the end of the number, sweat was running from his temples down his cheeks.

The second song was slower. I looked over at Austin. He wasn't singing but he nodded along with it. He turned his head toward me when he felt my eyes on him, but I couldn't read his expression. His posture made him seem a little…embarrassed, maybe. The room was getting warm and sweat and perfume were mixing in the air.

After a couple more songs the musicians dropped the volume. Joab moved to the front of the stage. I thought he would give a sermon, but instead he started saying things like "Lift your hands, lift them up to the Lord" or "Can y'all feel His power? His presence is here tonight!" I suppose you'd say he was exhorting us. His words had almost a sing-song tone, like each phrase was a lyric in a song he was making up as he went along. Every time he said something, a few people in the audience would respond with an "Amen" or a "Thank You Lord."

He kept the patter up like that for fifteen or twenty minutes, and all the time the musicians were vamping, and the people had their hands in the air and swayed, some of them moaning. I think the whole place was in a kind of trance.

A middle-aged woman in a green dress stepped out into the aisle with her eyes closed and everybody got real quiet, the musicians dropping down to barely audible but still keeping the beat going. The woman began to chant, something that sounded like "Aleihum aleihan salakium" and so on, for nearly a full minute. She didn't seem to notice the world around her. After she was done she blinked her eyes open like she was waking up and stepped back in her row. Joab shouted, "Praise the Lord! He is with us tonight!"

With all the people packed in, dancing and rocking and singing, it was now becoming oppressively hot. On the stage, the armpits of Joab's shirt were dark with sweat. I wasn't real sure the Lord was with us but I do know the place was getting claustrophobic.

My mouth was dry and the sweat and perfume were now joined by body odor in an almost overwhelming miasma. I was thinking about heading for the door for some air when Joab spoke again, his voice low and breathy. "I know there is someone here tonight who needs forgiveness," he called out to us in his sing-song voice. "I know there's some people here tonight who done wrong. Maybe there's even some people here tonight that don't know who Jesus is. If anybody here tonight has ears to hear and a heart to receive, I want you to come on forward."

One lady in a tanktop and silver hoop earrings went up and fell to her knees in front of the stage. Joab stepped down and put his hand on her shoulder.

"Thank you Lord. Thank you for moving this woman to change her life." He held the microphone away from his body and said some words over her. She shook and shivered under his touch.

"But I know this lady is not the only one here tonight who needs the forgiveness only Christ Jesus can provide," he continued. "I know there's more of you who need to come to Him. Maybe one among y'all is a lamb who's lost his way. Maybe one a y'all is tired of the Devil leading your lives. Or maybe, just maybe, a young woman was led here tonight so she could she turn her life over to Jesus."

A couple of ladies in the row ahead of us looked back. "Is he talking about me?" I whispered to Austin. I wiped away a drop of sweat running down my cheek. Austin didn't really do anything, just stood there fidgeting and didn't make eye contact with me.

Joab was still preaching. "It's come to my attention there is a certain young person here tonight, finding herself in a strange town, wondering what she's doing here. Well, let me tell you, she was brought here for a reason: so she can turn her life over to Jesus." It was obvious Joab's description didn't apply too widely. Lots more people were looking at me now.

I stepped into the aisle. Somebody nearby said Hallelujah, but I didn't head to the front. I turned and marched straight for the exit, shoving the pushbar with both hands. The metal door swung open and slammed closed behind me, cutting the music off completely. Outside I pulled cool air into my lungs like I'd been drowning.

A couple minutes later Austin came out. "Hey."

"Hey," I said. "It was a little stuffy in there."

"Yeah, it gets pretty hot." Austin ran a finger along the layer of dirt on the building's tan metal siding. "Look, I'm sorry. I didn't know he was gon' do that. It being your first visit and all."

"Your dad has a real way of welcoming newcomers, doesn't he?"

Austin nodded without looking up. "Sometimes I hate bein' the preacher's kid."

We stood for a minute while the June sun slid behind the treeline. "We can go on in my truck, if you want," he said. "I'll take you home."

Once we were on the road questions started spilling out of me. Everything had been so strange and I was trying to make sense of it. "What was all that in there? What was that lady saying in the foreign language?"

"She was speakin' in tongues."

"Could you understand her?"

"Nobody could understand her," Austin said. "It was a different language."

"But do these people believe all that? Speaking in

tongues, like it's the fourteenth century or something? Do they really think God made her do that?"

Austin's face turned a shade darker. "Yeah, they really think that."

"But that's ridiculous," I said. "I mean, how could that be real? She was just making it up. It's not like she was speaking Spanish or anything. Isn't that weird?"

"Why would she make it up? Maybe it's weird to you, but it ain't such a big deal here."

"But why did she do it? You think God really wants her to talk like that?"

"Listen, Dani. Don't you think God works in people's lives?"

"I don't know," I said. And I didn't. "But I'm pretty sure if He does, His goal isn't to make some random lady talk like a fruitcake or have people handle snakes or whatever was going on there."

"There wasn't no snakes there," Austin said in a low, slow voice. "We don't do that."

The last few minutes of the drive passed in silence. I glanced over at him but the brown eyes didn't meet mine. His hands were tight on the steering wheel. We pulled up to my house and I stepped out of the truck.

"See you on Saturday?"

"I reckon so." Austin reached over to pull the passenger door closed and drove off. It occurred to me that I must have offended him.

CHAPTER THREE

Dad was driving Ryan and me on the twisty little roads that had brought us to Adelaide. A gut-encompassing sickness curled me in a ball in the cramped backseat of Dad's '69 Ford Mustang.

"How're you doing back there?" Dad asked.

I opened an eyelid but the rush of trees outside the window just made things worse. I closed it again and groaned.

"Look, Dani, there's a scenic look-out a mile ahead. We'll stop there and you can switch seats with your brother."

"What? No way!" Ryan said from the passenger seat, actually looking up from his little screen.

"Your sister's car sick and needs to sit in the front." Dad laid a hand on Ryan's leg. Ryan shrank away from him. "Be a good sport, okay?"

"It's not fair! She's not supposed to get the front seat 'til we stop for gas!"

"Don't argue with me, just do what I say for once," Dad said, voice raised a little. I felt bad for him. He'd tried hard to stay cheerful the whole trip but I could tell he might be cracking. Not that I was helping in my current state of queasy agony. "Ah, here it is." He pulled off the road with a crunch of gravel under the tires.

"What are all these people doing there?" Ryan asked as he opened the door.

"I don't know," Dad said. "Looks like they're checking something out down below."

I reached weakly for the lever to push the passenger seat forward and stumbled out, wobbling for a moment before I found my footing. I thought I was about to puke but a rising breeze blew the staleness of the car from my face. The air here was crisp. The bile rising in the back of my throat went back down, like a boiling pot removed from the heat before overflowing. I swallowed and took a few steps.

A mini-van, a Cadillac, and a pickup truck were parked on the shoulder next to our car, their owners gathered in a knot next to a low stone wall. A breathtaking vista stretched before them, an Ozark wonderland of rolling, forested hills. Oddly, all their cameras were aimed down at something on the other side *of the wall.*

I tentatively followed Ryan and my dad, still not too steady on my legs. At the edge, I drew in a sharp breath. Ten feet down, on the trash-strewn grassy slope at the bottom of the drop-off, a huge black bear paced back and forth on all fours. A man with a baseball cap and wrap-around sunglasses reached out his hand and the bear stopped his pacing and rose, broad pink tongue lolling out as he looked up with greedy curiosity. The man dropped a chunk of food to him, then another and another, pulling off each piece with a sharp crinkling of plastic, the bear rolling his head from side to side to catch the morsels with his mouth. I looked closer to see what the man was feeding him. A package of Twinkies.

I stepped up to Mr. Shades without hesitating. "Hey, you shouldn't be doing that." I could sense Ryan rolling his eyes behind me, but I didn't care. Everybody knows you're not supposed to feed wild animals, especially junk food. I should probably be more prudent but I try live my life like Janis, fearless and independent.

"Ain't hurtin' nothin'," Shades replied without turning his head. It got real quiet as all the other people turned their attention to the confrontation. A heavyset woman put a hand on the man's arm. "Honey…." He shook her off.

"So what happens when that bear decides to climb up

here?" I asked him.

The man raised his head with a disgusted look on his unshaven face, his lips half-parted in a sneer. Keeping his gaze on me, he tore off a big piece of Twinkie and tossed it over the side with deliberate slowness. "You one a' them animal rights people? If you're worried about it, nothin's keepin' y'all here."

From somewhere behind me Dad said, "Come on Ryan, come on Dani, let's get going."

"But Dad, I want to see the bear some more," Ryan said.

"I said now!" Dad put one hand on Ryan's shoulder to keep him moving. A couple kids with sunburned faces and no shirts snickered as Ryan and Dad passed by. Probably the delightful offspring of the bear baiter.

I held my ground, glancing down at the bear. It turned its head up in my direction and its dark eyes locked with mine. Something simultaneously cold and hot went through my body, the way prey must feel when it's spotted by a predator. Out of the corner of my eye I could see the man freeze, his hand stopped in mid-air. The heavy-set woman moaned and said, "Oh my God, it is looking right at that girl." For a moment, everything seemed electrically charged.

I stared at the bear and it at me. I felt as if the bear were marking me somehow, like with a branding iron, only inside me instead of on my skin. And poof, just like

*that, the moment was over. It broke its gaze, fell down
on all fours, and ambled off down into the trees.*

———————————

I shook my head and opened my eyes, and I was in
my bed in the rental house. The air conditioner was
off and the only sound was cicadas outside the
window. Had that been a dream? It had
seemed…actual. Not dream- like at all. But that
hadn't really happened. Our actual car trip had been
so uneventful I had almost died of tedium.

"Weird," I said out loud, testing the reality of my
surroundings. Everything seemed normal. Probably
only an anxiety dream. I wrapped my blanket around
me and went back to sleep.

———————————

Aunt Eunice led Ryan and me sliding and skidding
our way down the steep hillside behind Springbloom.
She was sure-footed as a mountain goat, and I tried
to follow her lead. The trick seemed to be to grab
hold of an outcropping of gray limestone or a
scrubby pine tree on the descent, avoiding the
treacherous patches of loose red soil or dry branches
that broke off with a hard grip.

Halfway down Aunt Eunice steadied herself against a moss-covered boulder with her sinewy old hands and caught her breath. "Do you feel that, children?" she asked.

"Feel what, Aunt Eunice?" Ryan asked.

"Oh, I always get a certain feeling when I descend to the valley," she said. "I can't rightly describe it. This country used to belong to the Indians, you know. They believed this area was sacred ground."

And with that, we started off again. I love Aunt Eunice but honestly, she's a little crazy. She's the kind of person who sees weeds growing at the side of the road and stops the car to pick them for dinner. She only shops at the grocery store for meat and a few other things, and gets most of her food from her garden or on her foraging hikes. Her goal for our hike on this particular day was to pluck, pick, dig, or otherwise procure our own lunch out of Nature's cupboard. I just hoped Mother Nature's cupboard held fewer dangers than Aunt Eunice's deep freezer.

We were all too intent on avoiding twisted ankles and banged shins to speak any more until we reached the easier flat part leading into the wooded bottom land. We wore jeans and long sleeves to keep out the ticks and our nostrils were filled with the chemical sweetness of Deep Woods Off. The air became cooler and moister the deeper into the trees we went, and there were no sounds except our steps on the ground and a few distant twittering birds.

"Look there, kids, our first catch of the day," Aunt Eunice said, pointing at an open patch where a fallen tree let the sun shine through. Around the downed tree blackberry bushes grew thick and tangled, their berries hanging in clusters from the ends of the thorny canes. "I thought these would be ripe by now," she said, leaning over and popping one in her mouth.

The berries were plump, their sweetness tinged with puckering sour. Ryan and I filled our mouths and almost as quickly the basket we'd brought with us. "I'll fix these at lunch with milk poured over them," Aunt Eunice said. "And there'll be enough left to bake a pie tonight. No objections to that, I suppose." I made a sound in agreement but it was otherwise strangely quiet. Aunt Eunice looked around. "Now where did that boy get to?"

"Aunt Eunice, Dani, come look! Quick, come look!" came Ryan's voice from off in the distance. We pushed our way through underbrush to find him sitting on an old oak tree with an odd jog in its trunk, shaped and sized like a little seat. Ryan extended an arm toward us, cocking his head and squinting an eye as if looking through a rifle sight. "Halt! Or the sniper shoots you in the chest!"

"Huh. You've found the thong tree," Aunt Eunice said. "Been a long time since I've come across that."

"A what tree?" I asked.

"A thong tree. This is exactly the sort of thing I meant when I mentioned the Indians. They used 'em as markers, so they wouldn't forget where some important spot lay."

"So they made the tree grow like this on purpose?"

"Yes indeed," Aunt Eunice said. "When this tree was just a sapling they bent it over 'til it was horizontal, using a couple forked sticks to hold it down. But the tip of the tree turned upwards and continued growing. By the time the sticks rotted away, the tree had a permanent crook like what you see here."

Ryan fired a couple shots with his arm. "I took out the whole regiment," he reported. "It's safe now. You can sit here if you want, Aunt Eunice."

"Oh, I'll pass, honey," Aunt Eunice said. "But you know, there's a creek that direction. This thong tree points right towards it."

We followed where the trunk was pointing and sure enough, not more than a hundred yards away, the ground dropped away and a little stream ran trickling through the exposed roots of black walnut trees. Ryan had his shoes off in a hurry and splashed right in, scattering tadpoles and water bugs in every direction. I wasn't far behind him, stepping gingerly onto the uneven pebble bed and letting the chill water run tickling around my feet.

"My word," Aunt Eunice said from shore, "would you look at this wild sorrel! This will be perfect in the salad." She bent over and stripped the long oval leaves off the sorrel, tossing them in the basket on top of the blackberries.

"How did you learn all that stuff, Aunt Eunice?" Ryan asked from where he stood with his hands on his knees, eyeing a rock crevice where a crawdad was hiding.

"What stuff, dear?"

"You know, about thong trees and what plants to eat and all that?"

"Ryan, I have been walking these here mountains since before I was your age. I have learned that if you pay attention and give it respect, this land will reward you with riches."

Aunt Eunice picked her sorrel and Ryan poked around the crevice. And for a moment, there in the water under the walnut trees, I did feel something like what Aunt Eunice had mentioned. Not a church kind of feeling, exactly. Not like Austin's dad was trying to make the people feel. But something not too far from that, either.

CHAPTER FOUR

I was a little surprised Austin came to pick me up Saturday night after the church incident earlier that week, but he was true to his word. We walked down to the Cultural Center, the conversation a little awkward between us but not frosty.

Out front, a couple white-haired men in flannel shirts smoked cigarettes. "Got yourself a pretty girl there, Austin," one of them said as we went up the steps. Out of the corner of my eye I could see Austin give him a wordless nod.

Inside, the lights were darkened and the music was already underway on a raised wooden stage at one end of the hall. A young guitarist and an ancient fiddler played together under the stage lights for a couple dozen tables. The audience was a mix of ages, like at the church.

Teenagers sat laughing at a few of the tables, middle- aged and elderly couples clapped along politely with the music at others. At the bar dudes with burly gray beards and leather jackets drank out of clear plastic cups. The air was hazy thick with cigarette smoke.

Austin led me through the place. As we edged around a table, a slender man with long black hair and a black beard, maybe mid-twenties, tapped his arm. "Hey man, what's going on? Austin, right?" the man said, knocking the ash off a cigarette with his other hand. Austin mumbled affirmatively and the man nodded at me. "Who's the lady?"

"Her name's Dani," Austin said. "She's new around here."

"Yeah, I could tell." The man put out his hand without rising. I shook it. Long, delicate fingers. He had tattoos of Celtic symbols all the way up his arm. "Tristan's the name. Why don't you two pull up a seat?" He said it to Austin but was looking at me.

"Uh, sure," Austin said. He grabbed an empty seat from a nearby table and held it out for me. The gesture seemed overly formal in a place like this.

Another guy, younger, probably not much older than me, arrived at the table and pulled up a chair next to Tristan. He had on a red Razorbacks baseball cap and a cigarette in his mouth. He and Tristan wore matching white shirts with embroidered patterns on the sleeves and smocking down the front.

"This young troublemaker is Eli," Tristan said to me, gesturing to his younger companion. "He's playing with me tonight. Our first time together in front of an audience."

Eli nodded. The hair sticking out under his hat was sandy-blond and his face had a reddish complexion. He leaned back and checked me out for a minute before extending his hand. "Dani," he said, almost as if he were testing the name out in his mouth. "So. From up north. How'd a city girl like you end up in these parts?"

"How do you know I'm from a city? Or up north?"

Eli took the cigarette from his mouth. "I just know. Accent. But you got an aura, too. Different from folks around here."

"She's Doc Moser's granddaughter," Austin interjected. "Stayin' over behind the gas station."

Eli gave Austin a disdainful look. "Thanks," he said sarcastically. It seemed like there was some bad blood between these two. Eli turned his attention back to me. "Doc Moser's granddaughter. I bet you're real spiritual, ain't you?"

I laughed and glanced at Austin. He wasn't smiling. "You've got me pegged wrong there, cowboy."

Eli studied my face. "I don't think so. Let me see your hand."

He took it before I could respond and started tracing the lines on my palm. It tickled and I balled my hand, but he gently squeezed my wrist and my hand opened back up involuntarily, like one of those flowers that bloom in the morning sun. He rubbed the tip of his forefinger around the skin near my thumb. "You're very in touch with the things of the earth, Dani. A connection with nature."

I pulled my hand back. This guy's pick up routine was obviously well-rehearsed. "Really, I've never noticed that before. Almost the opposite in fact."

Eli smiled a little but when his gaze met mine his eyes were serious. The irises were palest blue. The fiddler and the guitarist on stage wrapped their song up. "You like this kind of music?" he asked me.

"It's all right. I'm really more into the blues."
"Good." Eli stood. "I reckon we're up now, Tristan."

"All right, let's hit it," Tristan said, stubbing out his cigarette. "You nervous?"

"Nah." Eli took a long look back at me. "Hope you enjoy our set. Maybe you'll hear a tune you like."

They grabbed some instrument cases from the back of the stage and sat down on metal folding chairs. I realized the embroidered shirts were their stage costumes. Eli pulled out a guitar. Tristan picked up an hourglass- shaped stringed instrument and put it on his lap.

"Hi, we're the Gin Soaked Boys," Tristan said into a microphone placed in front of his chair, and they started to play. I might not have been too familiar with the music, but I could tell they were good. Eli had a high voice, surprisingly beautiful, and Tristan harmonized with him in a lower, rawer register. I didn't recognize the song but it sounded old.

> They captured me on King's River, boys
> I might'a killed the crowd
> Except I wore that ball and chain
> Ringin' so clear and loud
> My ma she came and poured scorn on me
> She said to shut my jaw
> 'Cause there never been a wickeder man
> In the hills of Arkansas.

Eli strummed the chords, and between verses Tristan plucked out intricate, hypnotic patterns. I leaned over and asked Austin what the strange instrument was. "A dulcimer," he answered. "You never seen one before?"

"I've never even heard of one before." I watched Tristan's fingers move up and down the fretboard. It sounded kind of like a guitar, but its tone had an echoing, almost droning quality that reminded me a little of Indian music. I was completely sucked in and when the song ended I actually jumped, jolted back into the real world. I knew then why I'd come here this summer and it was this.

"I'd like to dedicate the next song to a girl named Dani," Eli said into the microphone with a wink in my direction. Still flirting with me, even from the stage. He whispered something to Tristan and they started to play, bluesy, with Tristan coughing out the lyrics in the hoarsest voice he could make. After the first line I laughed out loud.

"What's so funny?" Austin asked me.

"The music. It's on old Etta James blues song. *I'd Rather Go Blind.*"

"I don't know it."

"I do. I listen to this all the time. How do you think Eli knew I'd know this one?"

Austin shook his head.

The Gin Soaked Boys finished their set and disappeared. Austin and I sat at the table without speaking. He seemed to be picking a hangnail on one of his fingers. I tried to start a conversation. "So, how'd you like the music?"

"Fine, I guess."

"You must know all the songs they play here."

"I've heard 'em."

"So you listen to this all the time?"

"I mostly listen to rap." Austin seemed to be

studiously avoiding eye contact. He was cute but I was wishing he had a little more, I don't know, verve or something. Maybe down in these parts they'd call it gumption.

"Really? Rap? I'm surprised to hear that." He didn't say anything back. This wasn't going too well. He couldn't still be upset about the other night, could he? An elderly lady with a guitar took the stage and started warbling some song, mostly off-key.

I told Austin I had to visit the ladies room, but really I was looking for Tristan and Eli. I had to talk to them about their music, tell them how it had moved me. And I had an additional idea besides that. Back behind the bathrooms, the door at the end of the hallway was ajar, a conversation drifting in from outside. I recognized Tristan's voice and took a peek. Gravel, dumpster, some buckets. I stepped out and saw Tristan and Eli sitting on a couple crates. Eli hurriedly put his hand behind his back.

"Oh, it's you," he said when he recognized me. He pulled his hand back around, holding what I first thought was a cigarette. Its paper was wrinkled and unmarked, and the smoke floating out of it had an oily, spiced odor. I realized it was marijuana, though I'd never seen it before. Eli handed off the joint to Tristan. "Spare crate here, if you want a seat."

Tristan took a deep drag and held the smoke in his

lungs for long moments before raising his head and slowly blowing it out in a long trail. "You want some of this?" he asked me in a slightly hoarse voice.

"Um, maybe. I mean, sure," I said, hoping I sounded nonchalant. This wasn't what I'd come out here for, but I could hardly say no. Not with what I was about to ask them. So I sat on the free crate, told myself I'd head back in to join Austin in a minute. I took the joint from Tristan and put it to my lips. I tried to suck it in but nothing happened.

"Breathe in with your nose and your mouth at the same time," Tristan instructed. I did it and the smoke entered my lungs, hot and acrid. I started coughing.

Tristan laughed. "It's the same for everyone their first time."

"So you can tell it's my first time?"

"Hey, at least you actually inhaled it. Eli here practically burned up my whole stash before he got the hang of it." I laughed at that and relaxed a little.

Eli grinned. "So did you like our tunes?" he asked me.

"I loved it. I can't believe you sang Etta James."

"You know Etta James?" Tristan asked, eyebrows raised.

"Yeah. I listen to her on my Ipod all the time. But it was so cool to hear it like you guys do it, bluegrass style or whatever."

"Yeah. The thing about her is, the songs are so solid you can really do them in any style." Tristan passed the joint to me again. "Another hit?"

I managed to keep the smoke in for several seconds this time. It felt active in my chest, like something alive.

I passed it on to Eli, who sat hunched over with his elbows on his knees and his head down. "So you guys sounded great in there," I said. "But I think you two are missing only one thing."

Eli grinned. "Yeah, what's that?"

"A female voice."

"And I guess that'd be you, right?"

"Damn straight," I said. "And I could play guitar with you too."

"Right, we don't need no three-chord strummers."

"No, I'm good. I really am."

"Are you now?" Eli raised his eyebrows. "What do you think, Tristan?"

Tristan looked me up and down and turned back to Eli. "Listen, young buck, we need to practice for the festival so we have more than two songs to play. If you think we can do it with another member, that's on you."

I felt my stomach tighten a little. He meant the music festival from the poster.

A strange little smile stole across Eli's face, like he just caught on to something. But maybe it was just the pot. "So, Dani, you gon' be around here a while?"

"The whole summer," I said. "Give me a date and I'll check my calendar." I giggled at my own stupid joke. The pot was not helping me keep my composure.

"And you ain't afraid to play in front of people? Like, a lot of people?"

"No," I said. "I can do it. If it's cool with you and Tristan."

"It's cool," he said with a chuckle. "It's definitely cool." Nobody spoke for a long time after that, just a warm breeze and some crickets singing and us passing the joint around. I felt more relaxed now than I'd ever felt before. We were in our own little world, just the three of us, and time slowed down to the speed of the smoke slowly rising in crazy looping shapes.

I don't know how long passed but it was a shock, an intrusion, when someone appeared from the other side of the dumpster. "Dani," a voice said. I looked up. It was Austin. Oh, God, I'd kind of forgotten about him. Maybe I'd assumed he'd find someone else to hang out with. Okay, truthfully, maybe I'd ditched him in favor of somebody more fun. Our gazes met, and his eyes widened a bit as he recognized what was going on.

"Um, I don't think she's out here," he said to someone inside the door.

"Are you sure? Let's take a look." It was Dad's voice.

My insides clenched.

"Oh, shit," said Eli under his breath.

Dad stepped outside, glanced behind the dumpster. His face fell when he saw me and what was going on. And then, his features hardened, his eyes narrowed slightly. "Come on, Danielle," he said with a calm voice that was worse than anger. "We're going home."

CHAPTER FIVE

"What am I supposed to do with you, Danielle?" My dad paced back and forth in the kitchen. He's a big pacer when he's upset. Judging from his frantic speed, he was absolutely pissed. "Lock you up for the summer?"

"No," I said, more sullen than I intended. I slumped in the chair. The only light was the one over the sink, and my dad's shadow loomed huge against the wall out in the hallway.

"It's not even the pot. Honestly, that's not the big deal. But Christ, Dani, we've only been here a week, and already you've found the same kind of crowd you were running with back home. I mean, what are you going to be doing when we've been here a month, shooting up heroin?"

"No, Dad, I'm not going to be shooting up heroin. It's not like that."

He stopped pacing and glared at me. "Oh, what is it like, then?"

"Nothing. You know I didn't want to come here in the first place."

His pacing resumed. A sleepy voice came from the darkened rear of the house. "What are you guys doing out there?"

"Go back to sleep, Ryan. I'm having a talk with your sister." He paced a few more times, stopped in front of me, and leaned over. His voice was low but hard-edged, almost hissing. "And what am I supposed to tell your mother about this?"

I ran my finger along a crack in the wood of the kitchen table. "I don't know. I thought you two were barely even talking."

"Oh, we'll be talking about this, I can promise you that." Back again to the pacing. A chorus of cicadas outside crescendoed and died back down. Dad's shadow glided along the wall, matching him step for step.

"If it's such a big deal, I'll just go back to Eden Prairie and live with Mom," I said. It actually wasn't a very good threat. Now that I was going to play at the music festival, in front of people, like I'd always dreamed about doing? No, going back had suddenly gone from fervent desire to the last thing I wanted to do. Sure I wanted to see my friends again, but my friends could wait.

Dad shook his head. "No way. If you can't be trusted to go out for a couple hours in Adelaide, how can we possibly trust you to be without supervision the whole day back home?"

"If you trusted me, why were you checking up on me, anyway?"

"Checking up on you?" Dad pounded the kitchen counter with his fist. "I went out for a walk, Danielle! That's all. Little did I know I can't stroll around for fifteen minutes without finding you doing something illegal."

"So one slip up and now it's like I'm a criminal."

"Are you kidding me? One slip up?" Dad stopped, took a deep breath, and closed his eyes. He opened them again after ten seconds and pulled up a chair to the other side of the table. At least the pacing was over. I slumped down further in my seat, trying to evade his stare.

"Danielle, I'm worried about you. Your grades fell all year, you missed your curfew repeatedly, sometimes we went whole weekends without seeing you or knowing where you were. We caught you hanging out in a bar."

"It was a blues club, actually. And I wasn't

drinking." I kept my face neutral but grinned inwardly. The trouble I'd gotten in had been worth it to see Minnesota's best Janis Joplin tribute band.

"You were underage and you weren't supposed to be there. That's the point. I was hoping a summer off would break some of your patterns." He ran a hand through his hair, straightened his glasses. "Oh, Christ. It just occurred to me. I have to call Austin's parents and tell them about the marijuana."

"No! Austin didn't have anything to do with it!"

Dad looked confused. "But I thought you went down there with him?"

"I did, but he didn't know about what we were doing."

"So who were those guys you were with?"

"They were playing music on stage. I started talking to them afterwards about playing guitar and stuff out behind the dumpster."

Dad's mouth fell open. "So, you just met some strangers and started doing drugs with them?"

"No, they weren't strangers. Austin knew them. And they were musicians. We connected right away. I knew they weren't going to hurt me or anything."

Dad was shaking his head. "You didn't know anything about them. Do you realize how dangerous that could have been, Danielle? And if Austin was such good friends with these guys, why wasn't he there with you?"

"I kind of…ditched him."

Dad's face fell even further. Apparently my ability to disappoint was limitless. "I guess that explains why I found the boy moping around on the sidewalk out front. Well, thank you for being honest about that, at least." He rubbed his forehead. "Just…go to bed now."

I slowly brushed my teeth and closed my bedroom door behind me. I laid there for a few minutes, my eyes welling up in the dark. After a few minutes there was a knock at my door, so quiet I thought it must be Ryan. "Come in."

But when the door opened it was Dad. "Can we talk a bit more?"

I turned my face away from the light in the hallway so he couldn't see my red eyes. "I guess."

He sat on the side of the bed and the imprint of his weight pulled my body towards him. I rolled closer to the wall.

"I don't know," he said. "Maybe I'm not being fair. I probably shouldn't say this, but it's not like I never smoked pot in my day."

Okay, that part was interesting. I turned my head back just enough to see him out of the corners of my eyes. "Really? You smoked pot?"

He chuckled. "Sure. From time to time." He

looked at something on the floor, like he was reviewing something in his mind. "You know, Dani, this isn't how I pictured our summer. I wanted, I don't know, a fresh start for you. For all of us. After Mom and me splitting. Losing my job. Putting the house up for sale. I know things haven't been easy for you and Ryan."

For the first time I noticed Dad had little lines in the skin of his face. Had they always been there? He looked really, really tired. I felt kind of sorry for him, actually. He had always acted like everything that had happened was just a small patch of hard luck and would straighten itself out. I hadn't ever thought before that he might really be feeling bad.

He shook his head, as if straining to keep his eyes open. "Well, it's late. We'll figure things out in the morning." He got up and paused at the door, looking at me one last time.

"Good night, Dad," I said.

"Good night, Dani." He closed the door softly and shuffled down the hallway to his bedroom.

The next morning I woke up early. Normally I would've gotten up and turned off the A/C before settling back under the covers, but not today. The smell of Dad's coffee wafted through the house and I heard his voice on the front porch. I padded down the hall in my socks. The front door was open and I could hear his conversation clearly through the screen. He was on his cell phone, his free hand holding his mug. Judging from the tension in his voice, Mom was on the line.

"Please, you think I don't remember what pot smells like? Jesus, Deborah, who do you take for me?... Of course I keep an eye on her.... Yeah, but she's almost sixteen years old. She's not a criminal, I can't lock her in her room like she's in jail.... I'm irresponsible? You've got to be kidding me! You're the one up there doing God knows what, deciding if you can still stand to be with me..."

I went back to my bed and lay on top of the blankets for a long time. It was freezing in my room but I didn't care. I could hear Dad's voice outside the house, rising in anger, lowering to a snarl. It didn't sound like he and Mom planned on getting back together. It didn't sound like I was helping things either. I rolled over on one side and felt tears run from my eyes onto the pillow.

———

Aunt Eunice came over after lunchtime. I'd stayed in

my room all morning. I guess I was sulking. Ryan had been outside, whooping or something right outside my room, but I hadn't bothered opening my window to yell at him to stop. Just lay in bed and felt guilty. I mean, I wasn't exactly sorry for the night before. I hadn't hurt anybody. But maybe some of the things I'd done had been kind of stupid.

Most of all I felt guilty because I'd let Dad down. He and I hadn't spoken again and I wasn't sure if I was in trouble or not. The one time I'd seen him in the hallway he'd just looked sad. When Aunt Eunice arrived, he came back to my room, knocked lightly on the door.

"Yeah, come in," I said.

He opened the door a crack and leaned his head in. "Pack your stuff, Danielle. You're going to stay with your aunt."

"What? For how long?"

"I don't know. A while. Just pack up, all right?" He closed the door again. I heard him sigh in the hallway.

I took all my clothes and everything out of the closet and dresser and threw it all in the corner and screamed. I didn't even know why. I was angry at something: Dad, this stupid town. Probably me most of all. And then it was over and I picked all the clothes and put them in my suitcase and my backpack, along with iPod, my *Sandman* books, drawing pad, charcoal and pencils, toiletries, my guitar in its hard case. I carried out the guitar case and backpack to Aunt Eunice's truck.

To my surprise, Ryan went in the house and came out with my suitcase. It was going to be a relief to be free of his constant noises and annoyances. So why didn't I feel relieved? "I'll miss you," I said to him.

"You're just gonna be at Aunt Eunice's," he said, dropping my suitcase by the back bumper. "You'll still see me all the time."

"Yeah, I guess. Don't let the zombies get you while I'm gone."

He rolled his eyes. I reached to hug him and he pushed me away. "Hey! What are you doing?" He darted off into the trees, making noises like a machine gun.

Aunt Eunice came out and gave me a smile. I smiled back weakly and climbed in the passenger seat, and we were off, Aunt Eunice driving like a dive-bombing hawk down the little backroads. It struck me Dad hadn't said good-bye. Was he that mad? Or did he think I was?

"Honey, I guess you're in some trouble with your daddy," Aunt Eunice said.

"Yeah, that's an understatement. He doesn't even want me around now."

"Actually, I'm the one who suggested you come live with me. I thought it'd make things easier for everybody. I hope you don't mind."

"Oh," I said. That made me feel a little better about things. "I don't mind. It's just, I don't want to be trouble for you or anything, you know."

"No trouble. It'll be nice havin' a little company. You can stay at Springbloom all summer, if you have a mind to. You work in the garden mornings, wash your own clothes, help me a bit around the house, and the rest of your time is your own. Deal?"

"Sounds good to me. Deal."

Aunt Eunice hesitated a moment, taking her eyes off the road to glance at me before speaking. "Dani, far as I'm concerned, you're old enough to make your own mistakes. Don't make a difference what I think anyway. Anybody who's determined to do something is gon' do it, no matter what her daddy or me or anybody says."

She seemed to be expecting an answer. "Yeah, you're probably right."

"Just don't do anything to worry me, all right? And you can call any time and let me know if you ever need help."

"I'll do that." I nodded. I'd pretty much screwed things up with Dad and Mom. Austin too, now that I thought about it. If we'd had a family dog, I probably could've added him to the list. Hopefully with a little effort I could go the summer without messing things up with my aunt, as well.

PART TWO:
GET IT WHILE YOU CAN

CHAPTER SIX

My room at Springbloom was the studio tucked in at the very top of the A-frame house, accessible through a trap door reached by a wooden ladder from the second floor. The room's walls sloped down because it was right under the roof and there was a private little deck out back. Aunt Eunice warned me it got hot up there in the summertime but if I opened the window at one end and the door to the deck on the other the cross-breeze would keep things cool enough. It seemed just about perfect to me. That first night I unpacked, imagining all the nights I would spend sitting out on the deck playing my guitar under the stars.

The next morning as I was eating my toast in the kitchen there was a knock at the front door. Ruskin was barking before I could even get up. Did Aunt Eunice really get many visitors all the way out here? She had already gone down to the garden so I answered it, and was doubly surprised to find Eli standing there.

"Oh, hi," I said, blinking.

"Um, mornin'," he said back, looking just as baffled as I must have. He had on faded bluejeans, a checkered shirt, the same Razorbacks hat as the other night. He put one finger to his temple and narrowed his eyes questioningly. "Is... is Eunice around?"

"Yeah, she's out in her garden. I can go get her," I said, stepping out. But right at that moment, she came around the side of the house, carrying bundles of vegetables and herbs in her arms.

"Oh, mornin' Eli. How's your daddy feeling?" she asked him.

"Better lately, thank you ma'am."

"I believe you two know each other, isn't that right?" she said. Without waiting for an answer she strode into the house.

"Yes ma'am, we've met," Eli said after her, turning a little red. He kind of half-smiled. "So you're livin' here, huh?"

"That's right. Up at the top." I pointed to my window, under the eaves.

"Cool," Eli said, nodding. "You must have pissed

your old man off bad havin' to move so quick."

My aunt came back out and handed Eli a large paper sack filled with various greens and a smaller paper sack folded over at the top. "Here you are. And some extra vegetables from the garden, too. Tell your daddy I'm praying for him."

"Thank you ma'am, I'll let him know." Aunt Eunice went back in the house and Eli walked with deliberate slowness over to his red Dakota Sport pickup.

"Hey, Eli," I called.

"Yeah?" he said, turning around.

"Hey. Um, I was thinking maybe you could help me out a little on the guitar sometime. I mean, I play pretty well, but you're really good."

"Yeah. I might could do that."

"And we've got to get ready for the show."

"Yeah, that too." He nodded.

"Great. How about tonight? If you're not busy."

"Tonight?" He half-closed his eyes. I wasn't sure what that meant.

"I mean, we can do it any time."

"No, tonight's fine. Get off work at six today." He opened the door and pushed the paper sacks to the passenger seat.

"Okay. Where do you work?" I asked as he climbed into the driver's seat.

"The Pig. Stocking. See you tonight." He shut the door and drove off. I watched his red truck kick up dust down the long gravel driveway until it disappeared around the first bend.

Aunt Eunice's garden greened half an acre of Ozark hillside and required constant weeding, watering, digging, hoeing, shoring up of berms and terraces, and general fuss. Tending it would be my job for the summer. It was late morning and I was in the zone, pulling up weeds like a champion among the endless rows of tomatoes when I sensed somebody standing near me. I wiped the sweat out of my eyes and raised my head. It was Dad, holding a manila envelope in one hand.

"Hi," I said with a grimace. I was gone one day and he was already checking up on me?

"Hi. Aunt Eunice said you were down here."

"Yep. Here I am."

"Look, I know you're not in the mood for me bothering you, but I brought you something. Your grandfather left it for you."

I didn't say a word, just blinked at him. I was curious though. He handed the envelope to me. It had my name written in cursive on the front. I recognized my grandfather's handwriting from the Christmas cards he'd always sent Ryan and me. I tore open one end and emptied its contents into my palm. A necklace, its delicate silver chain threaded through a shiny black...something. The something was crescent-shaped, about three inches long, and curved to a wicked point at the end.

"What is it?" I asked, dubious.

Dad leaned over and inspected it. "A bear claw, I think."

I ran a finger along the claw. Smooth and hard like enamel. Its black surface faded to a yellowish-brown along the bottom edge. "Isn't this really more up Ryan's alley?"

"It had your name on it. Your grandfather meant that for you."

"Where'd he get it?"

"Good question. But I hardly spoke to the man for twenty years."

I undid the clasp and put it around my neck. "Well, thanks for bringing it."

"You're welcome." Dad stood there, fidgeting with the keys in his pocket.

"So," I said. "I guess Granddad must have been an interesting guy."

"I suppose you could say that." A drop of sweat ran down my temple. I brushed away a couple bees buzzing around my ear. Dad bit his teeth into his lower lip. "You know I love you, Dani."

"Yeah, I know Dad." He just stood there without saying anything, looking at me with a half-smile on his lips, as if afraid to let me out of his sight. Because he couldn't trust me? Or because he couldn't bear to see another member of his family fall out of his life? Whatever, I wasn't the one who'd made arrangements for me to live in another house. "I'll see you sometime, all right, Dad?"

"Sure. Okay. See you sometime."

I knelt down and got back to weeding, listening to his retreating footsteps. When he was gone, I pulled the necklace out and held it in my hand for a minute. The motor of the Mustang started up in the distance. I squeezed the hard, sharp point of the claw, indenting the skin on my finger. What would it be like to feel it tearing through your skin? I shook my head and moved on to weeding the cucumbers.

Eli arrived that night after Aunt Eunice and I had eaten dinner. She insisted he have a plate of elderberry flower fritters and Eli didn't turn her down. He was still wiping powdered sugar from his lips as I led him up the wooden ladder and showed him my place.

"Cool room," he said. He nodded at my guitar, upright on its stand. "Alvarez acoustic. Sunburst design. Sweet axe."

"Thanks," I said.

"You say you're pretty good?"

"I'm working on it. I know some blues licks."

"Let's hear it."

I picked it up and sat in a chair, strummed a few chords. He sat across from me. I'd been working on *Sunshine of Your Love* and played the opening riff.

He bobbed his head a little. "Not bad. Here, let me take a crack." I handed the guitar over. He ran his fingers over the body, plucked the strings, and proceeded to lay out one of the smoothest blues lines I've ever heard. He smiled slightly and looked up.

"Huh. You're a lot better than me," I said.

"I get in a little practice. But you wanted to learn somethin' like what me and Tristan do, right?" He pulled out a pick from his shirt pocket, one with a little curved part attached to it. He slid the curved part over his thumb and picked out a pattern. "You see what I'm doin'? First the thumb pick, then the fingers, alternating. It's called finger-pickin'. You play the melody of the song low with the thumb, keep the rhythm with the higher notes. Like this." He played something that sounded like it was straight from

Johnny Cash.

He handed the guitar back to me with the pick. I hooked it around my thumb and tried to imitate him, but I messed it all up pretty fast.

Eli laughed. "Takes some practice to get the feel. Here, let me help." He stood behind my chair and put his right hand on the strings. "You fret the notes, and I'll show you how to pick it. Give me a G chord." I fingered the chord and he slowly plucked out the pattern. I felt his breath on my hair. The veins in his hand danced as he moved his fingers across the strings. "You get that? Try it slow."

"Maybe, I'll give it a shot." I tried it again, slow, and it was better this time.

"Yeah. You'll get 'er if you keep at it." He stepped back. I was sorry he wasn't close to me anymore.

"What's that around your neck?" he asked.

"Oh, this. It's from my grandfather. I think it's a bear claw." I took the necklace off and held it out.

He took it and held it between his fingers. "Most definitely a bear claw."

"Weird, huh? I wonder where he got it from."

"Probably Indians. He might've bought it from one, or it could've been a gift."

"But I don't know why he left it to me. I mean my brother's totally into dead animals and stuff. It doesn't make sense that it'd be for me."

"That's not how I figger it." I looked at him blankly. His face was serious, almost solemn for a moment while he examined the claw. When he spoke again his voice was different, mature, like he was reciting from a book. "For Indians, the bear was a symbol of motherhood. You know, protecting her cubs. And a symbol of healing, too. Definitely a good thing for a female. A bear claw like this might protect you. Keep you from harm. Or it might enhance your, um, feminine powers."

I smiled to hear him talk like that. He seemed almost like a teacher. A different side of him.

"You laughin' at somethin'?"

I didn't say a word. I had the feeling remarking on it would shut Professor Eli down faster than anything. Best to say something neutral, maybe a little admiring. "Wow, you really do know about Indian lore," came out of my mouth. Oh man, couldn't I have found something that didn't make me sound like an airhead?

"It's a hobby. No big deal." He reached over and dropped the necklace in my hand, his finger lingering on my palm. I smiled up at him and his hand closed over mine.

"So is it working?" I asked, setting the guitar aside with my free hand.

"Is what workin'?"

"The claw. Is it enhancing my feminine powers?"

"It damn sure must be." He leaned over and pressed his lips against mine. Traces of powdered sugar on my tongue. I dropped the bear claw to the floor. The windows were open and the insects outside played a symphony while we kissed.

We stood on the front porch, Eli needing to get home but neither of us wanting to separate.

"You busy in the afternoons?" he asked, brushing the hair from my face.

"I should be free." That was an understatement. I had absolutely nothing to do out here.

"Tristan and me are probably gettin' together later this week. Play a little music. Might be some other folks there too. No big thing."

I smiled. "Right. We need to start practicing for the folk festival, right?"

"Mmm-hmm." He put his arms around me. We kissed good night for the last time and let our touches linger until he finally pulled himself away and walked to his truck.

Aunt Eunice had already gone to bed so I went up and practiced finger-picking for a while. When I was sleepy I turned out the light. The air had turned cooler and I was about to close the door to the balcony when my ear caught a rustling in the trees outside. I stepped out silently.

There was no moon, nor could I hear anything above the song of the insects. As I was about to go back in a twig broke somewhere not far from the house. I squinted and thought I could just make out a dark shape shifting behind a clump of trees near the house, an ink blot flowing over a black page.

I stood peering. Had I really spotted something or was I going crazy? An itch developed on my chest. I reached in my t-shirt to scratch it, expecting to find a bug or a mosquito bite, and found only the bear claw, hot against my skin. Suddenly, barking came from below. Ruskin had discovered the visitor. The dark shape fled into the woods with a crackling of underbrush.

Ruskin stopped barking and the only noise was the endless singing of the crickets. The bear claw, which I still held in my hand, cooled. Strange. I returned to my room and rolled myself under the quilts, soft with age, that Aunt Eunice had made up my bed with. I replayed the evening with Eli in my head until I lulled myself to sleep.

CHAPTER SEVEN

Tristan's place was one of the ranch houses in a little residential neighborhood behind Adelaide's commercial district. Well, it wasn't exactly the house itself. Eli and I got out of his truck with our instrument cases in hand and took the footpath around back, down the flight of moss-covered concrete steps, and knocked on the door of the basement apartment. That was Tristan's place. It probably didn't get sunlight except an hour each side of high noon but I don't think it mattered to Tristan.

He opened the door wearing jeans and a tight black t-shirt, a cigarette in his mouth. "Welcome to my lair," he said, motioning us in with a nod. Inside consisted of a kitchen and a front room with a bed in it. About a thousand science fiction paperbacks were scattered everywhere and half a dozen instrument cases littered the floor.

Eli stepped over to a ratty couch where a dude in baggy sweat pants sprawled. "Corey, my man," Eli said. "Where you been hidin'?"

Corey was long, African jungle-cat long, and skinny almost to the point of skeletal. I was afraid his arm would snap when he pushed himself up to a sitting position. He did some sort of complicated fist bump with Eli and turned to me. When he spoke, it was with a baritone voice like a saxophone. "So, you're the latest paramour," he said with a flourish of his hands. "Eli does prefer the dark-haired beauties."

I raised my eyebrows. "We're not an item just yet."

Corey only smiled like he knew something I didn't. Jungle-cat long, and jungle-cat smile.

Tristan picked up his dulcimer from the bed and started fiddling with the tuning pegs. "So you two eaten?" he asked Eli and me. "We could go get something."

"Nah, we ate at the store," Eli said. "You?"

"I'll just smoke. I can eat later."

"You work at the gravel mine all day and you ain't hungry?" Eli asked.

"I'm not hungry right when I get home, young buck." He looked up from his instrument. "Shall we get started?"

Eli and I opened our cases and got out our guitars. I found a place on the edge of the bed and Eli leaned against one of the armrests, hat pulled down, guitar slung low. We started tuning up.

"So she cool?" Corey asked Eli, rolling his eyes in my direction.

"Yeah, go ahead," Eli said.

Corey pulled some papers and a baggie out of his pocket and carefully sprinkled the contents of the baggie into the paper.

"When are we headin' up to Batestown again?" Eli asked him.

"Sometime, but let's confer on the subject later," Corey replied in a low tone.

Eli snorted. "What the hell for?"

At that moment a toilet flushed and the door to the bathroom opened. A blonde girl stepped out, pretty and made up just so, wearing a plaid mini-skirt and perfectly matched blouse.

"Oh, good, I thought I heard another girl out here," she said. She held out her hand and I took it. "I'm Emily. I hope these boys weren't talkin' behind my back."

Her tone didn't sound like a joke, and for a second things could have gone either way, but Corey started laughing and then we all did, and Emily sat next to him. I noticed throughout the evening Emily would bite her lip and take sidelong glances at Corey to see if he was looking at her. He never was.

Corey finished rolling the joint and passed it around the room. When my turn came I pulled the smoke into my lungs much more easily than the first time. The room grew hazy with smoke and heat from all the bodies.

I picked my guitar back up and practiced my fingerpicking for a few minutes. Eli nodded along while I played. "Gettin' better," he said. "You been practicin'."

"Will you guys teach me the song you played the other night?" I asked. "The one about the outlaw?"

"The outlaw?" Tristan said.

"She means *Harrison Town*," Eli said. He came over and showed me the chords and another fingerpicking pattern. We played it together all the way through a few times, and Tristan came in with his dulcimer. I think the marijuana helped because I was pretty relaxed, even though I'd never really played music with other people like this. Eli even came in with a snatch of the lyrics at one point.

They captured me on King's River, boys
I might'a killed the crowd

We sounded pretty nice together, actually. Or, we would have, except I kept flubbing one of the stupid chord changes.

"Slow down, little bird," Tristan said. "Let's take that part real slow, and we'll speed it up later." So we did it slow, and it was better, but I still didn't hit all the notes right.

"Oh, shit," I said. "I'm sorry I keep messing it up."

"No worries," Tristan said, flicking his wrist away as if to sweep the worry away. "This is how it always goes at first. Anyway, time for a break. I've got a gift for all you lovebirds."

"I reckon I know what it'll be," Eli said.

"Do you now? Well, keep it a secret for the ladies."

Tristan went digging in his closet and came out with two metal rods, each about eighteen inches long. We followed him up the stairs and over a split rail fence into the field behind his place. The sun was behind the tree line and fireflies blinked out their Morse code messages from the darkening fringes. The mountain air was dry and cool, so unlike the humid summers back home.

Eli and I sat on one of the hay bales dotted across the pasture, Corey and Emily another. Tristan tossed his t-shirt in between us and jogged out into the field. He put his hands on his knees, as if gathering his strength or concentration. The Celtic tattoos covered his arms and his entire back, but his chest and belly were pale. From a distance, he looked like he wore a shell, a skinny armadillo of a man.

"What's he going to do?" I asked.

"Watch," Eli said. "You'll see."

Across from us, Corey sat behind Emily with his arms wrapped around her midsection. She learned her head back against him with her eyes closed. "What's the deal with those two?" I whispered.

"Corey 'n' Emily? I wouldn't worry about them. They break up 'bout every other week."

"They don't seem to have much in common," I said.

"Her parents don't like him, but that only makes them two even tighter."

Tristan adjusted something on the rods and raised his arms above his head, holding the rods crossed in an X. Their ends were on fire. He started spinning them, slowly at first, then faster and faster. The flaming ends twirled around so rapidly it looked like two solid wheels of fire. He fell to one knee, now spinning them above his head, now at his side, now crossing each other. Again to his feet, and then leaping in the air, or leaning back from his waist with his arms held straight up, always with the rods spinning perfectly.

The night was darker now and the circles of flame danced across the field. Tristan tossed them in the air and caught them again with perfect grace, above his head, behind his back, under his legs. The afterimages on our retinas created the impression of a sort of cage of flames around him. Watching the performance, I felt goose bumps rise on my arms and moved in close to Eli. He put his arm around me. Probably it was only the pot, but right then I felt as close to him as I'd ever felt toward another human being. I never wanted the feeling to end, and Tristan obliged, dancing on and on, his lithe frame leaping, twisting, bending, and rolling. And then, at once, the flames were out and he stood before us holding the rods in one hand, sweat sheening off his body. He bowed and we all applauded him.

"Now I'm hungry," he said, grinning. "Let's go eat."

It was late when Eli got me back to Aunt Eunice's. I was about to get out of his truck when he said, "Hold on one sec." He fished around in his jeans pocket and pulled out a crumpled up piece of lined paper. "Yeah, here you go."

I took it and unfolded it, smoothing it out. Bits of guitar tablature unspooled across the top of the page, depicting three or four guitar riffs in the same finger-picking style Eli'd showed me before. At the bottom were lyrics with chord changes marked over the words.

> *Hangman, slack your rope a while*
> *I think I see my brother coming a-many mile*

"What is it?" I asked him.

"It means you passed the audition."

"I didn't even know I was auditioning."

Eli grinned. "Well, you were. I knew you could play, but Tristan wanted to be sure. You know how to read guitar tablature?'

"Yeah, I can do that." When had he had time to write this out at Tristan's? But I realized he'd written it before. He had faith in me.

"It'll be a little tricky. You got to sing and play at the same time. Not just the chords, these riffs too, at the right time. You got to have it down. So practice."

"I will. Non-stop."

"Good girl." He leaned over and we kissed. "Now go on in before Eunice sets to worryin'."

Aunt Eunice sat up reading one of her mysteries and smoking a pipe under a pool of light in the great room. The smoke smelled good, like cherries. A moth fluttered around the lamp, casting huge shadows against the walls.

"Good night, Aunt Eunice," I said.

"Good night, dear." I started up the staircase. She called after me. "Dani." I stopped and turned. "You aren't in love, are you dear?"

"No. God no." I could feel my face turning red because that may have been a little bit of a lie.

"I'm glad to hear that." Aunt Eunice pulled the pipe from her mouth. "The Sutterfield boy's a charmer, ain't he?"

"Yeah, he sure is."

"Keep in mind, some of these Arkansas boys know a lot about charming the ladies but aren't so hot about acting the gentleman."

Aunt Eunice was a little old-fashioned, but I liked the way she was looking out for me. "We're just having fun," I said with more firmness than I felt. "It's no big deal."

"Good. I'm relieved to hear you're not falling head over heels." She took some tobacco from a pouch and packed it into the bowl of the pipe. "Do be careful with him."

"Thanks, Aunt Eunice."

"You're welcome, dear. Good night."

"Good night."

CHAPTER EIGHT

Eli and I stood ankle-deep in the chill water at the river's edge. "Git in," he said to me. "In front. I'll hold 'er steady." I gingerly stepped into the front of the canoe, awkward in my bulky life vest. The little craft rocked and bobbed in seemingly the opposite direction of wherever I tried to move my body. I flailed with my arms to keep my balance. A final unexpected thrust landed me on the front bench seat with a hard thud on my rear end.

I looked back to see Eli grinning at my predicament and I realized he hadn't held it steady at all. "Just get us in the water, you bastard."

He leaned over and put both hands on the edge of the canoe, his back and arm muscles flexing under his life vest as he shoved the boat, scraping along the sandy bottom until it glided free in the current. He pulled himself easily over the side, grabbed a paddle and guided us towards the middle of the river, and we were underway in the lazy flow of the White River. The plan was to float for a couple hours, stop and eat lunch, and continue on our way to the spot down the river where the canoe rental folks would pick us up.

Just upstream, Eli's father Enos had pushed in, riding with his buddy Marvin. Downstream, and already a quarter-mile ahead of us, several canoes held Eli's usual gang of friends—Corey and Emily, and others I hadn't met yet. I'd felt like the odd man out riding in the bed of Enos's pickup with the others on the way down, all of them finishing each other's in-jokes and surreptitiously checking out Eli's new girl from out of town.

"Wake up, Dani! Git your paddle in the water!" Eli yelled, frantically paddling. "We got to catch up!" I blinked and followed his command, dipping my paddle in and forcing the broad end through the water over and over until the lactic acid buildup caused my shoulders to burn. We reached Corey and Emily, and Eli skidded his paddle across the river's surface, sending a plume of water over the edge of their canoe.

Emily shrieked at her soaked jeans and Corey shook his dripping head, flinging water droplets off his hair like a wet dog drying itself. "You're lucky we're on the river or I'd come over there and kick your posterior," he called out in his deep voice. I would only have been mildly surprised if he could actually reach us with those long bony arms.

"I wish you'd try," Eli yelled back. "I'd be on you like a chicken on junebugs."

"You're a freak, man. You and that girl of yours, you're perfect for each other, 'cause you're both freaks." He waved us away. Eli and I laughed and laughed. It felt good to be in on the joke with him.

After that we relaxed under the late morning sun, letting the river push us along with only an occasional paddle stroke to keep us on course. The water burbled and the cicadas droned from the shore in swelling and receding waves of sound. Along the banks sycamore and black walnut let their overhanging branches dip down to the river's surface like fingers testing the water temperature. After perhaps a half hour, the trees gave way to steep bluffs, fifty or sixty feet high, banded layers of limestone in alternating shades of white, tan, and gray.

At a certain place he seemed to recognize, Eli steered our canoe right up to the face of the bluff. I reached out and traced my fingers along its coarse, cracked surface.

"What are we doing here?"

"Be ready," he said. "We're movin' slow, but it'll still be hard to see."

"Ready for what?"

He pointed at the bluff, several feet above our heads.

And then I saw.

Scratchy red lines, sketched or painted on the stone's surface. Outlines of lizards and fish. Four-legged creatures that might be dogs or wolves, but with human faces. Long snake-like figures with horned heads and triangle eyes, drawn as if emerging from fractures in the rock. The drawings were primitive, almost like a child's, but the pupil of an eye or a patch of fur or a precisely captured facial expression lent the figures an eerie realism.

A strange feeling came over me, as if I were seeing something secret, a code from another world. "Indian drawings." I breathed out.

"Yep. Indian art. Petroglyphs, they're called. A thousand years old. Here even before the Osage, who was around when the white men arrived." Professor Eli was back in class.

"Who are those guys coming out of the crack?" I asked, pointing at the snake-men. I didn't like them. They looked like they could actually see us.

"Hard to say. Some folks think they might

represent underwater spirits, coming out of the water to attack people and take 'em back down to their realm. But nobody knows for sure." Eli tapped a couple times on the rock. "And the Indians ain't exactly around to ask."

The canoe floated past the pictures and Eli let us drift for a while. I didn't speak. I wanted to hold onto that strange, spooky feeling of otherness, of a time past when man and nature were not separate things, and a spirit from the water could rise up and challenge an intruder on the river. I tried to imagine an Indian, before Columbus, climbing up on the face of the bluff to draw his pictures. What did he wear? How did he think?

Gradually I noticed a familiar smell wafting across the river. Shaking myself from my reverie I was surprised to see Enos and Marvin in their canoe smoking a joint, passing it back and forth while they floated. Eli steered us over to them. Enos wore a green fishing hat and dark glasses. His angular features reminded me of Eli's, but his skin was weathered, and his cheeks were drawn in, as if he didn't eat enough.

Enos passed the joint to Eli and he breathed it in, exhaling slow serpentine coils of smoke. "You want some?" he asked me.

I took it and brought it to my lips, carefully taking

it in the way I'd learned. Enos held his hand out. I passed it back to him.

"How y'all doin'?" he asked after a long drag. His voice was surprisingly rich for such a gaunt man. "Eli treatin' you right, Dani?" He passed the joint to Marvin.

"Yes, sir," I answered. "Like a gentleman." Had the word "sir" really come out of my mouth? Maybe Arkansas was starting to rub off on me.

Marvin smoked the last of the joint and flicked the burnt roach into the water.

"Strange to see the bluffs so high," Enos remarked, looking up. "You remember that year we had all the flooding? You remember that, Marvin?"

"Yep," Marvin said. Marvin wore a John Deere ballcap but no life jacket. His checkered shirt was unbuttoned down to his huge gut and he had a pack of cigarettes in his shirt pocket. "You want somethin' to drink?" he asked Enos, patting the top of the cooler sitting on the floor of their canoe.

"Nah."

"How about y'all?" Marvin asked, turning to us. "We got Cokes or Bud." I took a Coke and Eli a beer.

"You know, now I think on it, there was two big floods," Enos went on. "That one a couple years ago, and then that real big one about fifteen years back."

"Water flowin' through like a bat outta hell," Marvin said.

"Not like this year. Dry. Look how dark those bottom rock layers are. Used to bein' underwater."

"Be seein' a lot of bears later this summer," Marvin said.

"Yep." Enos sat in the bow of the canoe, his chin resting on a walking stick. Marvin sat back in the stern, resting with one hand folded across his enormous belly and the other gripping his beer.

I waited a couple minutes but it didn't seem like anybody was going to elaborate any further. "Sooo," I said. "Why would there be a lot of bears here this summer?"

"Oh, you know," Enos said. I shook my head. "When it gets real dry like this, they come out from deeper in the mountains. 'Cause they ain't got as much food as usual, you see. Normally they'd avoid a place with more people around, but hunger makes 'em desperate."

"Are there any bear attacks?"

"Oh, not usually," Enos said. "They's scared of people, you know, just like we is of them. But it happens sometimes."

The current drew us apart and soon Eli and I were back floating along in our own little world. Ahead of us, the others were landing their canoes on the sandy shore of a tree-covered island. Eli hopped out when we approached and pulled us ashore. It was a relief to get out of the life jacket and move freely again. His friends had already gotten a campfire going and were sitting around it. Marvin and Enos came in behind us. Eli and Marvin carried the cooler up onto the beach and soon we were all cooking hotdogs on sticks around the fire and drinking Budweiser in the hot sun.

I took off my t-shirt. The days working in Aunt Eunice's garden had already browned my skin nicely and I had worn my green bikini top and cut-off jean shorts. I checked discretely and was gratified to see Eli definitely had his eyes on me. His friends disappeared in pairs, off to make out or smoke pot, probably. I brushed my arm against Eli's and whispered to him, "Is there any place around here we can be alone?"

He smiled, almost shyly, and glanced at his dad. Enos and Marvin sat back against a couple trees drinking. "Daddy, Dani and me are going for a little hike around to check out the island."

"Go to it, boy. We'll probably be ready to go in an hour or so."

We walked along the beach before cutting across on a little trail through a thicket of trees. On the south side of the island broad stones stretched across the river, forming a series of rapids and waterfalls. "All this whitewater's why we're going by the north branch," Eli said.

I sat on one of the rocks, enjoying the heat of the sun on my skin. The water flowing by was so clear it looked like I could just reach over and touch the bottom, but when I plunged my hand in and stretched my fingers as far as they'd go the riverbed was still several feet down.

Eli sat beside me, his knees up to his chest. We exchanged glances and started kissing without a word. I pushed him back slowly onto the rock. I could taste the beer on his breath and smell the river in his hair. One of my feet dangled off the edge of the rock, cold water splashing against my toes, the other foot rubbing against his. Our hands were all over each other. I don't know how long we made out. Probably twenty minutes at least, our lips and hands and bodies intertwining. And then somebody came crashing out of the bushes. We both sat up with a jolt of surprise.

The interloper was Corey, out of breath and urgent. "Eli, Enos just collapsed. Fell right to the ground. You have to come quick." Eli leaped up and sprinted without a word or even looking back. Corey lingered a moment, probably noticing how confused I looked. "Sorry about that, Dani. You know Enos is ill, right?"

"No, I didn't know," I said, and ran a hand through my disheveled hair, but Corey was already after Eli. I hurried back the way we'd come.

Back at the beach, Enos was sitting up, waving everyone off of him. "I'm fine. Just a little weaker 'n I thought, that's all." His fishing hat was on the ground, revealing his bald, white head to the world. "Don't ever'body stand around and fidget. I said I'm fine."

Marvin picked his hat up and handed it to him. "I think we should git you to a hospital, Enos."

"I'll take you back Daddy," Eli said.

"The only thing wrong with me is ever'body makin' such a fuss. Help me up, son." Enos held out his hand and Eli pulled him up. Enos's face turned a little paler and for a second it looked like he was going to fall again, but he managed to steady himself. "All right. Let's get movin'. Eli, help me over to the canoe."

Once in the canoe's seat, he started issuing orders. "Marvin'll paddle me down to the landing point and Eli, you and Dani can follow us in your canoe. Jesse, Corey, you and your lady friends can go back whenever you got a mind to. The canoes is already paid for."

"Yes, sir," Jesse said. "We might as well come

along."

"Nah, the last thing I need is some big crowd of folks gawkin'. Y'all stay here and finish what's in the cooler. You can bring it by my place tonight."

The canoe trip back was quiet. For a long time neither Eli nor I spoke while we tailed Enos and Marvin. Eli avoided eye contact and mostly kept his head down while he paddled, as if he were checking something out in the bottom of the canoe. At one point he glanced behind him and our eyes met.

I risked breaking the silence. "I'm still practicing the finger-picking."

"Yeah? How's it goin'?" He turned toward me on his bench and seemed relieved I was making conversation.

"I've gotten it down it pretty good, actually."

Eli nodded. His eyes drifted. After a minute, he seemed to regain focus and spoke. "You know, I don't want you to get the wrong idea."

"About what?"

"I mean, my daddy smokes pot for his appetite."

I nodded, but wasn't really sure what he was getting at.

"He finished a round of chemotherapy a few weeks

ago, and he don't feel like eatin' without a little Mary Jane."

"Oh." I never know what to say after something like that. "I'm sorry he's sick."

"He's gettin' better. He's been a lot stronger the past couple weeks. But his appetite ain't caught up with him."

"No, it makes total sense. He has to eat to get better."

"I didn't want you thinking the wrong thing about him. It's been only me and him since Mama died." He lifted the paddle out of the water and held it across his knees. "Dani, I would do about anything to help him get better."

"I know you would." I smiled slyly. "So is that why Marvin smokes it too?"

Eli laughed and put the paddle back in. "Nah, Marvin's just an old stoner. He sure as hell don't need no help with his appetite."

CHAPTER NINE

Eli, Marvin, and I sat in the waiting area of the Batestown Regional Medical Center's oncology department getting seriously restless. There are only so many magazines you can read in those waiting room chairs that stick in your back in exactly the wrong place, only so long you can listen to the news on that television mounted on the ceiling and turned up just loud enough to aggravate your nerves, only so many times you can exchange awkward glances with your nervous, bored sort-of boyfriend and his family friend. And then, depending on your personality, your day, whether or not you had time to change out of your muddy clothes from canoeing, I guess if those things fall the wrong way, you go crazy. Eli certainly did.

But not quite yet. That was a little later, outside. First we were just sitting in those uncomfortable chairs, dirty, worried, bored, smelling mossy, when we heard Preacher Joab's voice booming down the hallway. "This the right level? You sure now, Austin?" Eli groaned a little bit and slumped down in his chair.

"Here they are!" Joab called out as he came around the corner, Austin a step behind. Joab's big brass belt buckle barely kept his red and white checkered shirt tucked into his loose-fit blue jeans. "Elishah Sutterfield. How's your daddy doing?" He strode up to Eli and held out his hand.

Eli stood straight upright and shook it. "He's fine, sir. Had a little spell, that's all." He spoke in an exaggerated tone of voice, but Joab didn't seem to notice the sarcasm.

"The docs say he gon' be all right?"

"Haven't heard yet. We're here to check. Better safe 'n sorry. Right, sir?"

"Amen to that. How you holdin' up yourself?"

"Fine, sir. As well as can be expected."

Joab looked around. "Afternoon, Marvin. Afternoon, Dani. Wish we could all be seein' each other again under a different set of circumstances." Marvin tipped his John Deere ballcap without otherwise moving and I smiled at Joab weakly. "We'd love to have you stop by the church this Wednesday, Miss Moser," he said to me. "We been missin' you there."

Before I could formulate an answer, a nurse came out to the desk at one end of the waiting room, probably to see what all the bellowing was about.

"Can I help you, sir?" she asked Joab.

"Is Enos back there? Can I go back and see him?"

"Enos? You mean Enos Sutterfield?"

"Enos Sutterfield. Yes, ma'am. I'm a close friend of Enos."

"Well, Mr. Sutterfield's undergoing some tests right now, but he—"

"I'd best get back there, ma'am. I'm his pastor. This is a time when spiritual support can mean a great deal to a man."

"Well, visitors aren't supposed—"

"Thank you, ma'am," Joab said, opening the gate next to the nurse's station and going through. "Just lead me to him." His booming voice receded as the nurse followed, protesting his invasion to no avail.

Austin fidgeted a little, his hands in his pockets. He glanced at me with his brown eyes and gave a little nod. I nodded back. Eli stood regarding us both.

"Sorry to hear about your daddy," Austin said to Eli softly, as if he were apologizing.

Eli gave Austin a contemptuous glance and spoke to me. "I'm tired of sittin' here. Let's go outside." He held out his hand, waiting for me to grab it. I did and we started off down the hallway. After a moment of indecision Austin followed.

Outside the hospital foyer, there were a couple wooden benches in a little grassy area, placed at a right angle to each other. Eli and I sat at one and Austin at the other. Traffic went by out on the highway beyond the parking lot. There was no shade and my clothes, now dried out, were stiff and itchy under the mean afternoon sun. Eli pulled out a cigarette and lit it.

A minute passed. Austin tapped his foot. "So, y'all together now?" he asked.

"Shut up," Eli said without looking up.

Austin's face reddened. "You got a problem?"

"Yeah, that's right." Eli still didn't look at him. "A problem with your daddy come charging in here like a big bad bull."

Austin stood up. A bead of sweat dripped down his temple. He spoke slowly. "He's here to offer comfort to a body in need. What don't you understand about that?"

"What I understand is, he's trying to rub off some glory on hisself or something whenever anybody else gets hurt." He blew out a long puff of smoke. "What you gon' do, standin' up like that? Sit your ass back down."

"Why're you with this rattlesnake?" Austin turned to me. "He ain't nothin' but trouble."

"You leave her out of it," Eli said. He threw his smoldering cigarette to the ground and stood. "She ain't your concern."

"She don't belong to you." Austin dismissed Eli with a wave of his hand. "This one here will lead you down the wrong path, Dani."

"I said leave her out of it!" Eli shoved Austin in his chest. Austin stumbled back but caught himself before falling. His face burned wine red under his dark hair, and Eli's fairer skin flushed pastel pink. They locked eyes and breathed hard, two lions sizing each other up.

"You got somethin' to say now, little boy?" Eli said. "Comin' up after your big bull daddy like his little calf. Comin' to harass some sick person so's he can get him and his little calf boy some better place in heaven. You got somethin' to say now, calf boy?"

Austin stared at Eli for long seconds without blinking, his fists balling. Eli stared back, a muscle in his cheek twitching. Five count. Ten. Twenty. And then Austin turned his back. "You can go to hell, Eli. You and your bald old man."

"That's it, you little turd," Eli said. He stepped

once and punched Austin in the back of the skull with a dampened thud, like a baseball landing in a mitt. Austin's head slung forward and snapped back. For a moment I thought he would drop, but he spun around, his eyes narrowed. A line of spittle ran down his chin. He drew in a sharp breath and raised his fists.

"Stop it, both of you!" I shouted, astonished to find myself rushing between them, my voice screechy. "Just stop it!"

They both put their hands down. Austin gave me a glance I couldn't read, but I think maybe pity, and he went down the sidewalk without looking back. Eli spat on the ground and glared at Austin's retreating form.

"Don't chase after him, please don't do it," I said to Eli, my face moist from tears. I was embarrassed by my own emotional response. Had I asked for tears? No, but I had them anyway. I put a hand on his chest. "You don't have to do anything, but don't chase after him."

Eli glowered until Austin turned the corner. He glanced at me and I thought his features softened a bit when he saw my face, but they turned hard again in a second. "Come on, ain't no use standin' here in the heat," he said and strode into the hospital foyer. I followed a few steps behind.

The trip back was tensely quiet. Enos was clearly spent, his eyes heavy as they scanned the highway. Eli was just as subdued, silent and brooding the whole way. I sat between them in the cab, hands in my lap, afraid to speak. Fortunately, the thirty-minute trip only seemed to last about six hours.

At his house, Enos walked to the front door with a deadened shuffle. Even taking the keys from his pocket seemed like a major effort. I waited by the truck, unsure of whether to come in with them. Enos called back without inflection, "You may as well come in, 'less you got somewhere you have to be. Eli kin take you home when you need to go."

It was getting a little late, but it was Saturday and Aunt Eunice had been expecting I'd be gone all day anyway. I followed them in, the screen door slamming shut behind me. The house was small and kind of flimsy. It smelled like stale cigarette smoke and old pizza. The main room had a couple worn couches, an old TV, five or six acoustic guitars, bongo drums, a banjo, and a small kind of stringed instrument that I think is called a mandolin. A fluffy white Persian cat stepped out and rubbed against my legs. I bent over to scratch her head.

"Her name's Iloka," Eli said. It was practically the first thing he'd said since the incident with Austin.

"Iloka," I repeated to the cat, stroking her fur. "What a pretty name you have, Iloka."

"It's Osage for cat. In case you were wondering."

I heard the crack of a can opening and Enos walked out of the kitchen with a beer. He opened the door to the back porch and went out without saying a word.

"Is your dad all right?"

"Not really. But there's nothin' we can do about it."

"Oh," I said, not really sure how else to respond. Eager to change the subject, I said, "So, aren't you going to show me your room?"

"Yeah, sure. Come on."

The blinds were closed but shafts of evening sun poked through places where the slats had kinked. When my eyes got used to the dimness I was surprised to see the room was full of books. A giant bookcase against the far wall was filled, and stacks stood by the bed, the closet, jumbled in a corner under some tennis shoes. I checked out a few titles on his bedside table. *Symbolism in Indian Art. American Indian Word Magic. Ritual and Magic Among the Mississippian Peoples. Seminole Medicines, Magic, and Religion.*

"Wow, you really are into Indians." I picked up the book folded open on his pillow. *The Broken Circle: A True Story of Murder and Magic in Indian Country*. "Is this a good one?"

"Yep," he said. "About some Navajos who was murdered in New Mexico. I started it a couple nights ago."

"Maybe I can read it after you're done." I sat on his bed. He fidgeted with things around the room.

"Yeah, cool. If you want. You need somethin' to drink?"

I shook my head. "So how'd you get so interested in Indians, anyway?" I took his hand and pulled him onto the bed beside me. He didn't resist.

"I don't know, I guess 'cause I'm part Indian myself, maybe."

"Really?" I scooted closer to him.

"Yeah, one-sixteenth. My great-great grandmother on my daddy's side was Osage."

"It looks like you're reading a lot about their magic." I brushed his arm with my elbow. His body relaxed a bit. "It ain't really magic. The Indians were in tune with nature, and they could use natural remedies like we use medicine."

I had been successful in drawing out the Professor. I liked the Professor. "You mean like herbs and things?"

"Yeah, herbs. But more too. Natural energies, sort of. Like they could draw power from nature to do things science can't explain now. But that don't mean it was magic. They just understood nature in a way we don't anymore."

"Cool. I still think I'd rather stick to hospitals though," I said.

Eli stiffened and drew away from me. Wrong thing to say. "Hospitals are bullshit. They never done my daddy no good."

"Oh. Sorry I brought it up." Maybe it wasn't too late to change the subject. I put my hand on his leg. "So, you want to…?"

"Nah. Not now. I mean…. I don't know. I want to be alone."

"Sure." Disappointing. The day hadn't turned out at all like I'd hoped. But I put that thought out of myhead. God, Dani, how selfish are you? I was upset because we weren't making out. How much worse had it been for him? "Can you take me home first?" I asked.

"Yeah. Let me get the keys."

It struck me there that despite my promise to Aunt Eunice, I thought I might be falling for him. Eli the professor, the guitar player, the boy who cared about his father. Falling for him because of those things, and despite the drugs and the temper and the sudden violence. But I knew that was a lie. For since the altercation with Austin I had not been able to put out of my head those fierce eyes, hard curled muscles, sweat and spit and passion. They'd scared me. What's worse, they'd also thrilled me, and I wanted to see them again.

CHAPTER TEN

Proudwood was the name of my grandfather's old house. I don't know why all the houses around Adelaide have names, but they do, at least the big ones. It was the first time Ryan or I had ever seen it and the place was enormous, though practically falling down. The windows were broken out, thick ivy climbed up the stone walls, moss engulfed the roof, and saplings grew out of broken places in the wrap-around porch. Inside the sagging fences of a side yard multitudes of bees flew in and out of the collapsing wooden frames of their box hives. Grandfather had spent the last years of his life in a nursing home and his house and beloved bees had gone untended.

"It is a shame to see the place fallen to such a

condition," Aunt Eunice said. "Proudwood was magnificent in its day. Six hundred acres of the finest land in the county and this house on a hill in the middle of it." She shook her head. "A true shame."

Dad only growled something unintelligible and stepped to the front door. He'd been grouchy all morning, probably because dealing with anything having to do with his father put him in a bad mood. The door wouldn't open at first so he had to give it a shove with his shoulder and then it swung in with a sudden crash. Ryan and Ruskin followed him eagerly inside with Aunt Eunice and me behind.

Ryan wrinkled his nose. "Smells bad."

"Yeah, like some animal died in here," Dad said, kicking an overturned chair out of the way with his foot. The place looked ransacked and stank with a mix of putrefaction and mildew. We explored the first floor for a while. It must have been opulent once, but now the long Persian carpet in the front hall was eaten through by insects, the fixtures in the kitchen rusted out, the great room filled with moldy couches and a grand piano with yellowed keys. "Stupid trespassing hunters," Dad remarked under his breath when he saw the empty beer cans spilling out of the huge stone fireplace.

One entire wall of the great room was covered with

floor-to-ceiling bookcases. I went over to take a closer look. Mostly medical books, it looked like. One book was sticking out a little. I pulled it, checked the title. *Essential Neurology for General Practitioners*. I opened it and half a dozen silverfish squirmed out. I screamed and dropped the book with a thud. "Sorry," I muttered as everyone turned to stare at me. "The book was full of bugs."

"That'll happen once the moisture gets in," Aunt Eunice said.

Ruskin barked from upstairs and we all climbed the broad, curving staircase from the great room to see what he'd found. In the hallway Ruskin had his head down, trying to get a paw underneath a closed door. Dad opened it and mice ran in every direction, disappearing into various dark corners and cobwebbed niches. A bed frame with no mattress was jammed into a corner, a dresser against the far wall, a desk under the window.

"This was my room," Dad said flatly. He gazed around for a minute. Bird calls came in through the broken window. "Hmm, I wonder...." He opened and slammed shut each of the desk drawers, frowning.

"What's in there, Dad?" Ryan asked.

"Mouse droppings. But, maybe over here?" he said, more to himself than us. He opened the closet door.

A couple moth-eaten shirts still hung forlornly. He reached up on the top shelf and felt around as if he were searching for something. "Aha!" he said, pulling down a little wooden box. "I can't believe it's still here."

"What's in there, Dad?" Ryan asked, practically leaping so he could see in, Ruskin jumping up beside him.

"Down, boy. Both of you." Dad looked into the box, blinking, a half-smile playing on his face. It was the first time the whole day his grumpy mood had broken. "Well, what do you know?" he said.

"What is it? What is it? What is it?" I wondered if Ryan was going to explode right there. I rolled my eyes, my heart scornful of his raring curiosity.

"It's Indian spearheads," Dad said. He shook his head, as if to wake himself from slumber. "Like arrowheads, but bigger. Found 'em all myself. When I was about your age or so." He handed the box to Ryan. "Want them?"

"Awesome, thank you!" Ryan took the box and pulled a dozen stone triangles out to inspect. Each one was about the size of a human palm. "Where did you find these? Are they real? Can you really put them on a spear? Do you think these killed any animals? How many Indians were there?"

"Slow down, son," Dad said, stepping to the desk.

"They're real, all right. There's a…" He hesitated, as if weighing how to phrase it. "A place near here where you can find 'em, or sometimes other Indian artifacts."

There wasn't much else to see and nothing to salvage anywhere in the house, so we soon found ourselves back out on the porch. The only ones still interested in the house were Ryan and Ruskin, who were running up and down the stairs exterminating a zombie infestation.

"Well, it's a true shame about the house. But we may as well start lunch," Aunt Eunice said. "Let me get the things from the car." She brought back a blanket and sandwiches and slices of tomato picked from the garden, and Ryan even settled long enough to stuff his face for a few minutes. After we had finished, she pulled out a little paper bag and passed out sassafras brittle.

"Mmm, delifious," Ryan said, actually drooling as he sucked on a huge piece.

"You're revolting," I said to him. "You eat like an animal." He crunched his piece and stuck out his tongue, covered in food chunks and trailing strands of sugary yellow saliva. I turned my head away. "I swear, you are absolutely vile."

"Do take care when you eat the brittle, Ryan," Aunt Eunice said. "Suck on it a smidgen first to soften it up, because it may be hard enough to take out a filling."

"I doan efen haff any filligs," Ryan replied, wiping his chin.

"Eunice, these are delicious," Dad said. "You certainly have the magic touch."

"In fact, Jim, I'll have you know your daughter made this," Aunt Eunice said. I tried to keep myself from smiling as I'd been keeping that part a secret.

"Cooking? My daughter? To whom do you refer?" He looked around the porch as if searching for another daughter who might better fit the description.

"Daaad, stop it."

"She picked the tomatoes too," Aunt Eunice said. "And grew 'em herself, mostly. She has absolutely worked wonders in the garden this summer."

"Well, I never would have believed it. Eunice, you've gotten more out of her in two weeks than I have in nearly sixteen years."

I almost glowed to hear compliments from Aunt Eunice and Dad like that. I hadn't had occasion to hear too many compliments from Dad lately.

"You know," Dad said. "Maybe I shouldn't sell the old place. We could come down next summer and fix it up here. Make it an annual thing. A summer house in the Ozarks."

"Well, you know I would love to keep Proudwood in the family." Aunt Eunice looked around at the ruin and overgrowth. "Be a lot of work to get it back in shape, though."

Just then I felt something hit the back of my head. I reached up and patted my hair. Sticky. What the hell? I heard giggling from behind me and whirled around.

"Oh my God, Ryan, I am going to kill you right now!" I jumped to my feet but he was already off into the house, Ruskin chasing after him in high excitement.

"Dani, what's wrong now?" Dad asked.

"That little brat threw a piece of the brittle in my hair! One that'd been in his mouth!" I could hear his steps as he thudded up the stairs. As if he could hide from me. I clenched my fists and shouted at the house. "I am going to come in there and rip your throat out!"

"Dani, I don't want to hear any talk like that!"

"I mean it! He has seriously signed his own death warrant this time!"

"Honey, calm yourself and let me have a look at your head," Aunt Eunice said. She ran her fingers through my hair, tried to disentangle the gooey, half-chewed lump. "Well, we can go on home and see if it will wash out."

Looked like lunch was over, and as usual, Ryan had managed to ruin things. And of course it'd been just as I'd made Dad proud for a change. I had never hated anyone more than I hated Ryan at that moment.

CHAPTER ELEVEN

The Piggly Wiggly on a weekday afternoon was not a happening place. The air rose in heat shimmers from the cracked, faded asphalt of the parking lot. There were only a handful of cars but Eli drove around and dropped me off behind the store.

"Wait back here a minute," he told me.

"You ashamed to be seen with me?" I asked teasingly.

"Yeah, it's the hair," he said.

Ouch. I pulled the ballcap I was wearing down further over my head. I bet Janis didn't have an idiot little brother ruining her beautiful tresses.

Eli must have realized from my expression he'd hit a nerve. "Manager don't want to see me walkin' in with no girls, that's all. I'll be back here real fast."

There was a metal cage behind the store holding

boxes and a forlorn grocery cart pushed against the wall. A used condom and some rusty RC Cola cans littered the ground. It was too hot to touch anything and the only shade was a straggly tree in a weedy patch next to a chain- link fence. I went and stood under it, but stepped right back away when a swarm of bees descended from a hive tucked under one of its branches. They buzzed in a little cloud for a minute before dispersing.

A corrugated metal door in the side of the building slid open. To my surprise, it wasn't Eli, but a girl in a wheelchair, wearing the Piggly Wiggly uniform: khaki pants and a white, button-down oxford shirt with a little cartoon pig over the pocket. She pushed the joystick on the wheelchair controller to roll out and gave me a hard look, like she was used to finding people back here and they usually weren't up to any good. "What the hell're you doin'?"

"Umm, I'm waiting for someone."

"Who?" She stared at me like she was trying to drill me into the ground.

"Eli Sutterfield."

Her expression softened and she even almost smiled. "Oh, you're the new girl. My name's Shea." She offered a hand and I shook it.

"Hi, I'm Dani."

"Christ almighty it's hot back here." She pulled a

pack of cigarettes out of her shirt pocket, tapped one out and lit it. "So you around for the whole summer?"

"Yeah, my dad has some business here he has to work out."

"Yeah, from your granddaddy dyin' and all," she said. I should have known I wouldn't have to explain myself. "Well, you certainly made an impression on the boys in these parts."

"Oh, really?" I said as nonchalantly as I could.

"Oh yeah, I got an earful about you from both Eli and Austin." Austin had given somebody an earful? Obviously she knew a different side of him than I did.

"It's strange the way everybody in town all knows each other," I said.

"Really? Guess I don't know no other way." She took a deep drag. "I been in school with Eli and Austin since kindergarten."

"Did they always hate each other?" I asked.

"No." She laughed. "In fact, they used to be best friends, if you can believe it."

"They were?" That would have been interesting to discuss further, but Eli chose that second to walk out the door. I smiled to see him in his store uniform and without his Razorbacks cap. His blond hair was an uncombed mess, but still cute, like a little boy getting out of bed.

"Oh, hey, Dani. I reckon you and Shea already met."

"We introduced ourselves," I said. "It took you long enough in there."

"Yeah. Manager was up my ass about bein' late agin."

"Jesus, what a prick," Shea said. "He schedules you for a ten-hour shift and throws a fit if you clock in two minutes past time the next day."

Eli shrugged. "Nothin' new. What were y'all talkin' about?"

"I'll tell you later. Let's get back inside," Shea said, tossing her still-smoldering cigarette to the ground. "You could sizzle grease out here."

Eli and Shea hid me in the stockroom while they went out to work, Shea to work the register and Eli to stock the shelves. Actually, Eli didn't get a whole lot of stocking done since every time he came back we made out for about five minutes. He brought me issues of *Guitar Player* from the magazine aisle to read while I waited in the buzzing of the refrigeration units.

I was leaning back against a big stack of canned

soup boxes and reading an article about soloing in the mixolydian scale when Eli sneaked around and tried to pull my cap off. I put my hand to my head and held it down. "Hey! I don't want you to see it!"

"Come on, babe, let me take a look," he said, sitting beside me. "It can't be that bad."

"You have to promise you won't laugh."

"I won't laugh." Eli's face was so solemn I couldn't help but believe him.

"All right." I sat up and slowly took the hat off.

His mouth fell open. "Oh my God! It looks like you been hit by a barber all hopped-up on meth! Christ, Dani, put the hat back on."

"You asshole, be serious. Does it really look bad?"

"I wouldn't treat my lawn the way your hair been treated."

I pushed myself away from him and put the cap back on my head with a pout.

"Come on, baby, don't be mad," he said. I pretended like I was reading the ingredients on a can of clam chowder. "What's wrong, Dani?" Eli reached over and touched my shoulder. I turned away.

"You know what's wrong."

"Oh, your hair's fine, baby. You know I was kiddin'."

I scooted back beside him. "God, I detest my brother. I swear I'm going to kill him."

"Bro's a little punk, huh?"

"Yeah, pretty much."

"Don't worry 'bout him. He'll get exactly what's comin' to him."

Looking back on it later, the way Eli said it was actually a little creepy. But I didn't notice at the time. "Really, how do you know?" I asked.

He put his arm around my shoulder. "Trust me." Just then we heard the door swing open and heavy footsteps stomped into the stockroom.

"Eli, you back here?" called out a man's gruff voice. Eli gave me an exasperated look and jumped up.

"Right here, sir."

"What the hell you doin' back there, boy, nappin?"

"No sir, I was jus'—"

"Fergit it. Grab the mop. Some kid puked over in aisle nine. That hyperactive kid who's here with his daddy twelve times a day buyin' gummi bears." I slapped my forehead. That could only describe one person: Ryan.

"Yes, sir."

"And if I catch you nappin' agin, I'll dock your pay. You're skatin' on thin ice today. You understan' me, boy?"

"Yes, sir."

The footsteps retreated and Eli poked his head around the boxes. "I'll give you three guesses which kid that is," he said.

"I only need one." I stood and approached the swinging doors separating the stockroom from the main part of the store.

"Hey, where're you headed?" he asked.

"I don't want you to get fired. I'll go hang out in town until your shift is over."

"I thought you didn't want to see your brother."

"I'll go out another aisle. They won't even know I'm here." I pushed through the swinging doors only to practically run Ryan over. Why he was standing in front of the swinging doors next to the dairy section I have no idea.

"Hey, Dani," he said, oblivious to the stare of icy, agonizing death I gave him. "Why'd you come out of that door?"

"Out of my way, you little brat," I hissed.

"Hey, Dad, Dani was in the back of the store, where the workers are," Ryan yelled loud enough for the whole store to hear.

"What's that?" Dad said, appearing from around a display of packaged cookies. "Oh, hi, Dani. Didn't expect to see you here. Did Eunice manage to get your hair fixed up?"

"Yeah, it's great. That's why I'm wearing a hat now." I felt the swish of air as the doors swung open behind me and then Eli was standing there, using a mop handle to push a wheeled bucket half-full of dirty water. "Dad, this is my friend Eli," I said, sighing. "He's the one I was telling you about earlier."

"Good to meet you, Eli," Dad said, giving Eli's outstretched hand a firm pump. "Eli what?"

"Eli Sutterfield, sir."

"Oh sure, Sutterfield. I know Enos, or did back in high school anyway. How's he doing nowadays?" My heart sank. Did Dad have to interrogate all my friends? And could he have possibly picked a worse question?

Eli wavered for a moment, but answered firmly. "Daddy's doin' fine, sir."

"Glad to hear it. Sorry I have to do this to you, Eli, but I'm afraid my son and I caused a little mess over by the cereal."

"I had too much candy!" Ryan blurted. "But don't worry, I feel better now."

Eli regarded Ryan coolly. "Ain't no big deal," he said after a moment, pushing the bucket towards aisle nine. "That's what we got the mop for."

"So how are you doing?" Dad asked, turning toward me. "Looks like you haven't had any problems making friends here."

"Fine, thanks," I said. "I was just headed out, though."

"Can I go with you, Dani?" Ryan asked. "Where are you going? Let me go with—"

"No!" I said, clenching my teeth and putting as much venom in my voice as I could. "You're not coming with me. I'm not even talking to you."

"Well, we'll see you around then some time," Dad said. "Maybe you could stop by and eat dinner with us tonight."

"Sorry, Dad, I don't think I can make it." I was already walking away. What I wanted to do most was go see Eli but I was afraid his boss would catch him fraternizing with me so I picked a different aisle. And besides, I kind of wanted to avoid the puke.

"See you," Shea said as I passed by the registers. "Maybe next time I'll tell you some Eli stories."

"Yeah, I'd like that," I called back. The automatic door opened and I stepped from the air conditioning into the heat like a wall. Another event ruined by my brother. Unbelievable. It may have been hot outside, but that was mild compared to the seething magma in my gut I felt against Ryan.

I heard somewhere the best cure for depression is getting out in the sunlight. Sounds like something Dad would say. But maybe it's true, because Aunt

Eunice had insisted I join her on a hike and I had to admit, it was helping. A day had passed and I was still smoldering over the hair incident. With our passage down from Springbloom into the valley I could physically feel my rage subside. All that was left was cold fury and a conviction that my brother would not live the rest of the summer.

I touched my hand to the spot on the back of my scalp where Aunt Eunice had had to cut away my hair. I felt like I practically had a bald spot. She saw me feeling around back there. "You know, dear, it really isn't too noticeable. It'll grow back before you know it."

"I'll have to wear a hat until Christmas, at least."

"You're being overdramatic, Dani."

"Aunt Eunice, just promise me one thing."

"What's that, dear?"

"Don't let me near my brother any time soon. Because I don't think I could stop myself from strangling him."

She looked back at me with a frown, was about to say something, but changed her mind. We continued down the path. The woods were busy around us, all calling birds and insects and swaying tree limbs, the air pleasant and mild under the forest canopy.

Aunt Eunice reached up and ran her finger along the feather she always wore in her hair. After a minute she said, "You know, Ryan reminds me of your daddy when he was the same age."

"Really?" I did want to hear more about this. Dad rarely talked about his childhood. "I can hardly believe that."

"Oh, he was impulsive, that's for sure." She laughed out loud. "I used to babysit him and had the most terrible time. Not able to sit still a minute, always off somewhere gettin' into something he wasn't supposed to. He's mellowed with age, but you can still see the old impulsiveness now and then."

"You can?" I was trying to reconcile this observation with the man I knew who wore a suit to work every day, until he'd lost his job at the real estate office, anyway. The man I'd never heard use a swear word harsher than darn or dang it, or maybe the occasional Jesus Christ. The one was always haranguing me about my homework or hanging out with the wrong crowd or talking back to Mom. This man was impulsive?

"Oh, certainly. I mean, to just up and take the kids down to Arkansas for the summer without any warning, even though he's only been here twice in twenty years. Don't you think that's impulsive?"

I let that bounce around while we stepped over a fallen log. "Yeah, I guess I see what you mean." She had a point, and now other memories flooded my brain. All the times he'd taken Ryan and me out for ice cream when it was supposed to be bedtime. The sudden purchases, the unplanned trips, the kittens or gerbils or parakeets he'd walk through the door with. Or the 1966 Ford Mustang that had pulled into our driveway one day without warning, Dad grinning at the steering wheel as he pulled up. He really was apt to do anything sometimes. It was something that'd always driven Mom crazy.

Aunt Eunice went on. "He always used to make your grandfather so aggravated, up and going out whenever he took a notion to. Didn't matter about school nights or church or chores. Oh, there was no stopping him. If Ben locked him in, why Jim'd disappear out the window of his room. They had the worst arguments about it. And one time they had one real bad one, when Jim was seventeen—not much older than you—and then he really did up and go and never came back."

A bobwhite quail called in the distance. I thought about Dad leaving home at seventeen. Not much older than me. And the same age as Eli. I tried to imagine myself leaving home and couldn't quite picture it. "But how'd he live on his own? What did he do?"

"He must've made his way somehow. Later on he sent me a letter saying he'd gone up North, to

Minneapolis of all places, and not long after that he met your mama. I guess it's no surprise he married her out of the blue. They'd hardly been dating two or three months, I think."

"My mother says it's the craziest thing she ever did," I said.

"Probably was," she said. "You're more like her, I think. Dogged. Headstrong. Goin' after what you want no matter what. But I do see a touch of your daddy too."

"You do? How so?" I couldn't help smiling at this idea. Me like him?

She held aside a branch as we went by a narrow place on the path. "Oh, mainly in your willingness to pursue trouble no matter where it may take you."

Couldn't argue with that one. I suppose she had me pegged pretty well. We walked on a little ways without speaking. After a while the sky turned darker and you could smell the coming moisture in a sudden cool breeze.

"Best we turned back," Aunt Eunice said. "Thunderstorm's comin' on."

We didn't talk much on the way back. I was glad we'd gone. And maybe I even understood a little more about Dad, and Ryan too. But I still hadn't forgiven him.

PART THREE:
BURIED ALIVE IN THE BLUES

CHAPTER TWELVE

The remaining weeks before the Adelaide Folk Festival passed in a hurry. I gardened during the day and rehearsed with Eli and Tristan most nights. Otherwise, I was shacked up in my room drilling my guitar and vocal parts. My fingers were getting more nimble and I dared to hope I wouldn't totally embarrass myself at our performance.

It was the Thursday night before the festival when I found myself sitting between Eli and Corey in the cab of Eli's pickup, Eli driving like 100 miles an hour down the curvy ribbon of highway to Batestown. We passed the medical center and turned off the highway. A sign read "Welcome to Batestown, pop. 11,781," and the road broadened into an avenue overspread by huge white oaks and lined with big old Victorian houses. Around a curve we entered the commercial district. Eli pulled off a side road and parked in front of a bank. "Tough to find parking here," he said to me as he pulled into the spot. "We'll be walkin' most of the night. Hope you didn't wear high heels."

I laughed. "That doesn't sound like me." I had on my usual blue jeans and tennis shoes, though I had worn a white blouse, since we were going out. I'd left the top couple buttons undone, partly because it was such a warm night, mostly because I hoped Eli would notice. No jewelry except the bear claw necklace. "So what is there to do in Batestown other than get in fights at the hospital?" I asked as we spilled out of the truck onto the sidewalk.

"Well, the hospital's on the outskirts," Eli said, ignoring my reference to his altercation with Austin. "This here's the town itself."

"You've never been to Batestown?" Corey asked in his deep voice. He leaned back against the pole of a stop sign, his baggy clothes exaggerating his skinny frame.

"No, never. Should I have?"

"She's been holed up at her aunt's place all summer," Eli said. "Got too much dirt under her fingernails to go out." I elbowed him playfully and he gave me a little shove.

"Batestown's the place to go for a good time," Corey explained. "None of the small towns around here are big enough to have anything to do. So everybody heads to Batestown for the weekend."

"All right," I said. I doubted Batestown would compare to the Warehouse District in Minneapolis but saying so didn't seem like it'd win me any points. "So what are we doing here tonight?"

Corey folded his bone-thin arms across his chest. "My cousin's got his buddy in from Dallas for the summer," he said. "I heard the dude knows how to party."

"Cool. We'll check it out," said Eli.

"So should we hit that first?" Corey asked. "Go up and see if the party's rolling?"

"Nah, still too early," Eli said. "Follow me."

We started off. I actually liked the town right away. It was labyrinthine and mysterious, the main street zigzagging steeply up the hillside and intersected at all kinds of angles by jagged little lanes. Lots of stone buildings built right up to the sidewalk, little cafes and coffee houses and art galleries. Diners ate at tables outside and teen-agers skateboarded and older couples walked hand in hand through little pocket parks. It felt old, historic even, some place Mom and Dad would want to go antique shopping on the weekend back when they were still together.

My calves worked and stretched up the steep grades as we ascended through a dizzying series of alleyways and other shortcuts. We skirted the leafy fringe of one yard while up at the house some balding, middle-aged men with long hair sat playing guitars on their back porch, illuminated by lights from inside. Their singing was clear in the night. "If I Had a Hammer." Corey muttered something about the damn hippies stinking up the place. I couldn't help laughing but I was a little out of breath from the climb and it came out like a horse cough. Corey gave me kind of a weird look, which only made me laugh harder.

"Where's Emily?" I asked him when I'd recovered. "Isn't she coming tonight?" I was a little leery of an evening without any other females I knew to talk to. Not that I knew Emily well, but she'd at least be a familiar face.

"Nah, she had to work. Evening shift at the Dairy Queen."

"A night without the ol' ball and chain, huh?" Eli said.

"You got that right."

We continued up a sharply inclined alley and over a low brick wall to reach the backside of what looked like a hotel. Corey and Eli vaulted up onto the chest-high loading dock but I couldn't make it. They both laughed at me trying to scramble up.

"Very funny," I said, giving them a mock-hurt look. Eli took my arm and helped pull me over the side.

We sat on the edge in shadow, dangling our legs, our backs against a rack of folding chairs. A dim light burned above a metal door, slightly ajar, in the far corner. Light jazz wafted out through the crack, along with the occasional clinking of glasses or a woman laughing at the punchline of some joke or remark. A streetlight down at the bottom of the alleyway flickered on and off with a buzzing pop.

Eli pulled a baggie out of his pocket and rolled a joint. "Now that's the shit I was waiting for," Corey said. Eli licked the edge of the rolling paper and pressed it together. He lit it, took a drag, and passed it to me.

I inhaled deeply, smoothly taking it in and holding it. "I'm improving," I said with a giggle as I exhaled, holding it out to Corey.

Eli chuckled. "You don't watch it, by the end of the summer you'll be a real head."

We just sat there passing the joint for a while. I leaned way out over the edge and looked up at the building. White limestone, almost glowing in the night, rising six or seven stories into the sky. "I'm surprised this town would have such a big hotel."

"Oh yeah," Eli said. "Batestown used to be like this

rich resort town, where folks from Little Rock or Memphis would come up in the summer 'cause it was cooler here."

"Yeah, now it's all chi-chi," Corey said. He leaned back on his hands, his Adam's apple rising and falling in his long neck as he talked. "Painters and tourists buying knick-knacks and shit. Probably that's who's in there, having their little cocktail soiree or some shit like that." He nodded his head toward the metal door.

Eli snorted and smoke blew out his nose. "I can't believe you just used the word soiree. And chi-chi."

"Yeah. I know English, you damn redneck."

"And proud of it," Eli said. He pulled his Razorbacks hat down even further than usual.

I took another drag, pulling a cloud deep into my lungs. I definitely had the hang of it now. I blew out a long trail of smoke like a steam locomotive, watched it drift off into the dark. I noticed when I leaned back on the concrete, the world seemed to move in slow motion, but when I sat back up it returned to normal speed.

"What are you doing?" Corey asked with a laugh as I pitched forward and back.

"Nothing. Just testing things out."

"Your girl's a freak, man," he said to Eli.

"I'm not his girl. Not yet, anyway." I punched Eli

playfully in the shoulder. He brushed it off and gave me a look like he was humoring me.

"Is that right?" Corey said. "Hey, Eli? You remember those two chicks we met up here from Creekboro?"

"Oh, yeah," Eli chuckled. "Man, I'll never forget that."

I smiled to myself and took the bait. "And what made these two chicks so memorable?" I asked, keeping my voice nonchalant.

"Oh, they wanted to have a good time," Eli said, grinning and looking away at something over by the street light. "No big thing."

"Hell yeah," Corey said. "They totally let us feel them up behind the movie theatre. Bras off, everything."

"And what about Emily?" I asked, seeing if he could take what he dished out. "She must be pretty cool if she doesn't mind you getting a little extra on the side."

"You're full of questions tonight, aren't you?" he said, half-narrowing his eyes.

"So she's cool with it, then, right?"

"Shit, give him a break," Eli said. "Those two are practically married."

Corey kind of grunted. "What she doesn't know can't hurt her," he said, shaking his head. He took the last drag from the joint, his thumb and forefinger gently holding on to burn up the absolute last bit before he flicked it off into a bush. "That was just what I needed. You always have the best shit, Eli."

Eli nodded and smiled without saying a word.

"Y'all ready?" Corey asked. He hopped down without answering and I followed suit, relieved I was cool enough to land on my feet without stumbling.

Another calf-challenging hike and we came to his cousin's house almost at the top of the hill. It was down the end of a long crushed rock driveway, two stories and dark wood like a log cabin, with a wrap-around porch. Trees completely blocked the view from the road, giving the place a real isolated feel. There were a few cars parked out front, but oddly, the lights in the house were off and there didn't seem to be any music or anything.

"This is it," Corey said, standing on the first step up to the porch.

"You sure?" Eli asked. The only sound was the insect orchestra, playing its nightly song. The situation definitely felt a little weird. I put the tips of my fingers against my blouse over the bear claw. The cloth was hot like it'd just been ironed.

"Yeah, I been here plenty a' times." Corey looked around at us. "Don't act like y'all are all spooked or something."

I swallowed my trepidation and followed them up the porch steps. In the house it was hot as hell and bizarrely quiet. The walls seemed to shift and sway as we stepped down a darkened hallway. Being high had been more fun before we came to this creepy place. We went down a set of stairs and I clutched the railing so I wouldn't fall down the undulating steps.

It was a little cooler at the bottom, but not much, and a faint vinegar odor irritated the back of my throat. Moonlight leaked through gaps in the blinds in the room's sole window, casting crazy shadow shapes. Some sort of techno music pulsed from a tinny boom box in the corner. The whole effect was disorienting, especially since the room was filled with piles of dirty laundry. I put a hand against the wall to steady myself and was sliding down to a sitting position when I saw that the laundry pile closest to me had a face. My stomach dropped and my brain froze.

I had to sit blinking for a minute before the scene resolved in my vision and I realized the clothes were all people, except nobody was moving. Bodies were draped over couches and love seats, slumped against walls or lying on the carpet. Somehow that was even worse than before. Were they dead? The techno beat persisted and I couldn't clear my head.

And then I spotted the reason why: the needles

stuck in their arms, syringes still dangling from the veins. I shuddered. Jesus, each time I figured out something new, it was more horrible than before. What had Corey gotten us into? This was not a place I cared to be. I wanted to get on my feet but the music had invaded my brain and kept me from acting.

Eli leaned over and spoke in a low tone into my ear. "This is a little harder than I want to party." He paused a second. "Don't you think?"

His words brought me back to Earth. "Yeah, definitely," I mumbled back to him. I was surprised at his being, so, I don't know... protective?

"Come on, let's go," he said to me. I gratefully grabbed his hand and he pulled me to my feet before turning to Corey, who seemed as taken aback as we were. "Sorry, bro, I think we're gettin' out of here."

"Yeah, all right," Corey said. His tone was sober and serious. He nodded at a shirtless figure in a corner. "My cousin's over there. I'm just going to hang out and keep an eye on things."

"You cool here?" Eli asked him.

"Yeah, I'll just catch a ride back tomorrow. Sorry about how this turned out, man."

"Don't worry about it," Eli said.

I had to force myself not to run up the stairs and out the door. Outside in the blessedly cool air we headed back down the driveway, the stone crunching beneath our feet. I took Eli's hand and held it tight.

"So," I said. "Do you think he'll, um, shoot up or whatever?"

"Corey? Nah."

We were quiet for a while. The town seemed stiller, too, as we descended. "Does that happen much around here?" I asked.

"What, the dope?"

"Yeah."

"I guess that dude from Dallas brought it up with him," Eli said. "I seen meth before. Pot plenty of times. But never heroin."

We passed behind the hotel again. The lack of light jazz suggested the soiree had broken up. The night had taken a depressing turn, and I thought of something daring to turn the mood around. "I have an idea," I said, glancing up at the loading dock.

Eli lifted his hat a little and looked at me with raised eyebrows. "Yeah, what's that?"

"Help me up again."

He stooped down and held his hands out, creating a step for me to climb up on the concrete platform. I peeked through the metal door while he scrambled up behind me. I could spy a ballroom, all thick carpets, flowered wallpaper, and huge, dimly lit chandeliers. Very elegant looking. It seemed like everybody'd cleared out. There were dirty dishes stacked on a couple tables, a vacuum cleaner in the middle of the room with its cord unwound. But no guests or staff in sight. I opened the door and slipped in.

"Where are we going?" Eli said in a low voice behind me. Since I didn't know, I didn't say anything back.

The scents of shrimp cocktail and crab hors d'oeuvres still lingered, mixing with carpet cleaner and a sort of general old hotel mustiness. Flutes of champagne stood untouched on a table. I picked two up and handed one to Eli. "To us," I whispered.

"You're crazy, girl," he whispered back, and we both took a gulp. Sweet, almost like Sprite, but with a bite as it went down the throat. It was the first time in my life I'd ever drunk champagne. I got the feeling I could drink it a lot more often, though. I drained the glass.

"Come on," I said with an unintentional giggle. I wasn't sure if it was a result of the marijuana or the alcohol. I led us out of the ballroom into the corridor beyond. Not a soul around. I spotted a sign for the stairs halfway down the hall. Perfect.

We sneaked along, me tiptoeing and Eli right behind. The plush carpet muffled our steps. We reached the door for the stairs just as somebody came around the corner. A man in a blue suit with brass buttons and a hat. Probably the bellboy. "Excuse me, are you guests here?" he called out from the end of the hall, eyeing us suspiciously.

Eli gave me a grin. I pushed open the door with a slam. We were through in an instant and bolted up the wooden steps like we were being chased by a hellhound. Second floor. Third. Fourth. Fifth. We came to the landing on the sixth and top floor, stood for a moment with our hands on our knees catching our breaths. A door opened below us, and footsteps resounded throughout the stairwell. I counted the floors as the footsteps came nearer, trying as hard as I could to breathe quietly. At the fourth floor, they stopped and a gasping for air came up. A door opened and closed, and then it was quiet. Eli and I laughed.

There was another, narrower set of metal stairs here marked with a sign reading "Roof Access: Guests not Permitted." Of course we had no choice but to go up. The door at the top wasn't locked, just a turn of the knob and we were out on the roof. There was a giant roaring air-conditioning unit and a water tank, some wooden crates and a rusty pile of metal tools in one corner. A stone wall wrapped all the way around the top, about two feet high. And below us, the main drag of Batestown dropped away down the hill, occasional headlights going up and down, a yell or laugh floating up to us from little knots of pedestrians here and there on the street.

We didn't spend much time admiring the scenery. Practically as soon as the door closed behind us, our hands touched and grasped. The danger we'd been in pulled us together like we were magnetized. Our lips touched, tongues explored, hands free and all over each other. A slight dampness of sweat in Eli's curly hair, a touch of salt on his skin. His muscles hard under his t-shirt. The ticklish feeling of his tongue on my neck, his fingers tracing my spine. A slight breeze through my hair. Our kiss went on and on and I never wanted it to end.

But I stiffened when Eli's fingers tried to slip under my bra. "I'm not ready for that yet," I said in a low voice, opening my eyes.

He was silent for a beat before turning away. "Damn it," he said. "Don't tell me you gon' be like that."

"Like what?"

"You know what," he said. A neon sign flickered and buzzed on the top of the building across the street. "A cock-tease." His voice was accusing and hostile, a lot different from the protective tone he'd had at the heroin house. Apparently he only had that attitude when he thought he was going to get some play.

"I'm not a...a cock-tease. I want to wait a little longer before doing that."

He turned back towards me and roughly grabbed my shoulder. His eyes were triangles and fierce, his irises vertical slits, like a reptile. He pushed me down and I fell to the roof with a thud.

"Hey, what the hell do you think you're doing?"

He didn't say anything but was on top of me before I could react, his mouth on mine, forcing his tongue between my lips. One of my arms was trapped under his body. I pushed against him with my free arm but he was too heavy. He had a hand on my breast, moved it down to my stomach. His reptile eyes were on me but somehow not seeing. I shouted but it came out muffled inside his mouth, still pressed hard against mine.

Suddenly I felt a kind of power in my left hand. I reached with it and dug my nails into his face, raking them across.

"Son of a bitch!" he hissed, pushing himself off me.

I rolled over and pushed myself to a sitting position, rubbing the back of my head. A knot had welled up, sensitive to the touch. Something on my skin just above my breast itched. A scratch from Eli's rough handling? I gingerly touched it. Not a scratch. The bear claw. It was burning hot.

Eli slouched against the low stone wall, blood welling from three serious scratches across his cheek. Strange they should be so deep, because I kept the nails on my left hand trimmed to play the guitar. We sat for a few minutes, breathing hard, no words between us. I could feel my face wet with hot tears but I didn't brush them away. That would be an acknowledgement they were there, and I wanted to be harder than that.

"We should get your face cleaned up," I said when I was sure I could hold my voice steady. I held the still- warm bear claw between my fingers. "The wounds could get infected."

He glared at me resentfully. Blood ran down his cheek and onto his t-shirt. Then, he saw me holding my necklace and his expression changed. Something in his eyes registered and he looked as if he'd just realized something. He stood up.

"Come on, let's go. I'll drive you home."

"You're crazy if you think I'm driving home with you."

"What, you gon' walk forty miles back to your house? It's over now. You ain't got to worry. Let's go."

The walk back and drive home were as awkward as you might expect. In the truck, Eli drove with his head tilted to one side, holding in place an old t-shirt between his face and shoulder to stanch the blood.

"So. One last rehearsal tomorrow?" I asked in a flat tone as he pulled out of town and onto the highway.

He looked at me darkly, though the effect was kind of comical with his head tilted. "And you think we're playin' together again after tonight? Is that how you figger it?"

No. I wasn't going to let Eli back out now. Not after practicing every night. Not when I was so close to taking my guitar and really performing in front of people. Not when everything I'd worked for all summer was really about to happen. Would Janis give up now? Hell no.

Eli'd used me, or tried to, and I was going to use him now in return if I had to. I spoke with all the firmness I could muster in my voice. "On Saturday when you play, I am going to be up on stage with you and Tristan. You owe me that much, after what you did tonight."

I expected a hostile response, but actually, Eli seemed to crumble. "I don't know." A long pause.

"Tristan's strange. He don't necessarily want to play with a new person."

"That's not true. We've been practicing together for weeks."

Silence for the rest of the trip. He dropped me off at Aunt Eunice's. I slammed the passenger door shut but he rolled down the window before I went two steps.

"Hey."

"Yeah?" I said without turning around. I expected he was about to apologize. Moths fluttered in the beams of his headlights, casting flickering shadows against the house.

"I'll talk to Tristan. We'll work something out."

No apology.

"Good. You do that," I said without turning so he wouldn't see the fresh tears. "You know, you should really put iodine or something on your face when you get home."

He rolled the window back up without a word and drove off down the driveway. As he pulled away, I final turned and watched the tail lights recede into the thick humid night.

CHAPTER THIRTEEN

I had trouble sleeping that night. The world seemed tense. The air was too still. The singing of the insects, always soothing before, was now an irritation. And my head ached, not just the knot from Eli's attack, but deeper, a throbbing in my brain as the summer's events looped endlessly through my mind. Dad's catching me smoking pot and moving to Springbloom. The river trip and the petroglyphs. Eli and Austin fighting at the hospital. My grandfather's old house. Cutting my hair. And over and over again, Eli pushing me down on the roof of the hotel and my hand scratching his face. All these scenes played out hour after hour, torture because I wanted nothing more than for sleep to come.

It must have been two or three in the morning

when I felt the heat of the bear claw on my chest, followed by a rustling from outside. It was barely audible above the droning of the cicadas and at first I wasn't sure I was really hearing it, but the noise went on insistently.

I rose and went out to the deck but could see nothing in the moonless night. The crazy urge came over me to leave the house. In fact, more than an urge, it was a compulsion, like I couldn't really stop myself even if I wanted to. I climbed down the ladder to the second floor, deliberately, silently, feeling each hardwood rung under my bare feet in the dark house. Was I insane? What was I doing? But my limbs kept moving of their own accord.

Down the stairs to the first floor, stealthily into the kitchen. The front door creaked when I opened it. I hesitated, afraid Ruskin would start barking. Nothing. I slowly pushed open the screen door. Cool in the open air, refreshing against my skin. Moonless, windless night, darkness almost like a solid thing.

Down the porch steps, along the stone path, across the driveway, the bare skin of my feet pressing into the gravel. Where was I going? My heart beat faster. Into the trees, stepping through prickly pine needles, the intense piney fragrance of the woods enveloping me. Was the smell stronger at night or did I notice it more because of the darkness? I don't know how far I walked, surely a half-mile or more, and then the compulsion left me and I stood bewildered in the night. Why? What was here? And then I heard a sound that made my heart skip a beat.

Breathing. Not mine.

I turned my head slowly, confused, terrified, but curious as hell to find out what had brought me out here. A huge black mass towered over me, eight or nine feet tall. How had it gotten right behind me without my hearing? Especially with that breathing, in and out, ragged and moist. The dark mass reached out, placed a heavy paw on my shoulder, and I realized it was a bear: the biggest I'd ever seen. Not that I'd ever seen any this close. Oh, God, if this thing didn't kill me, I knew I was going to die of a heart attack because my heart was beating in my chest about two hundred times a minute.

I heard words, not out loud, but in my mind, plain and deep, starting in my head and resonating throughout my body: *Do not be afraid.* And after it said them I wasn't, not anymore. The words cleared my mind, relieving me of all the night's burdens. My heartbeat slowed. I exhaled and realized I'd been holding my breath in for a long time. My lungs felt clean as I let out the old stale air.

The paw on my shoulder was velvety, warm,

powerful. The bear leaned over, its snout inches from my face. Its breath was hot and damp, earthy, honeyed. It blew out and the air filled my lungs back up, expanding them to their limits, as if I'd never breathed in so deeply before. It was a little painful, actually. And then I exhaled again.

My breath gives you strength. Partake, for you will have need of it.

My eyes closed involuntarily and my body relaxed. I could feel the hot sweetness of the bear's breath linger in my chest, flow through my body, sending tendrils to every limb and extremity, healing, strengthening, energizing. And when I opened my eyes, it was morning and I was in my bed in the attic.

The summer folk festival in Adelaide attracted more people to that little Arkansas town than I would have thought the place could hold, and at least half of them seemed to be performers. There was the main stage at the Cultural Center, where acts were booked all day Friday through Sunday, but impromptu performances could break out any time, whenever a banjoist or upright bassist happened to meet the mandolinist or fiddler he hadn't seen for so many years and they decided on the spot to strike up a version of "Arkansas Traveler" or "Keep on the Sunny Side." It didn't matter where. The pavilion in front of City Hall. The sidewalk outside the music store. The parking lot of the Piggly Wiggly. Even, at least once, in the middle of the highway, backing up the only traffic jam I ever saw in Adelaide.

Twenty thousand people came from all over the Ozarks and beyond, carrying their battered instrument cases, their camcorders and camera phones, in a few cases even their mini 4-track recorders. And all this made my stomach queasy, because the Gin Soaked Boys with Special Guest (me) were scheduled at the Cultural Center, Saturday at 7PM, and every damn seven-year old or octogenarian walking in the street seemed to be able to pull out her guitar and pick it better than me.

It was just before lunchtime Friday and I was checking out the custom carved banjoes and fiddles for sale at a booth when I felt a hand on my shoulder. For some reason I thought it would be Eli and I jumped when it wasn't. "Oh, Dad! Sorry, I wasn't expecting you."

"Forgotten me already, eh?" He grinned, but it seemed forced.

"Of course not. What was your name again?"

Dad laughed. "You wouldn't happen to have seen

your brother, have you?"

"No, but he's the last person I'd be looking for."

"He said he was going out to play an hour ago and never came back. I know he just went off and wandered into the festival, but…" His voice trailed off.

I rolled my eyes. "I'm sure if he's been snatched it'll be about ten minutes before the kidnappers return him for being too obnoxious."

Dad's face fell. "You know, Ryan's really looking forward to seeing you play tomorrow." I had trouble believing that, but I kept the sentiment to myself. "Well, I'm going off to hunt for him. Give me a call if you see him, will you?"

"Yeah," I said. "I'll let you know if I spot the little twerp."

Dad shook his head and sighed at my comment before heading into the crowd. I wandered around a little, checking out some other booths, and spotted Eli and Tristan smoking cigarettes over by a gelato stand. Eli's face looked really nasty with the raw sores along his cheek. I decided it would be best to act as if nothing had happened and see how he reacted. I walked up and said brightly, "Hi! How are y'all?" just like a real Arkansan.

"Fine, thank you," Tristan said. "And how do you do this morning, little bird?"

"I bet she can't wait to play tomorrow, can you?" Eli said all friendly-like, to my surprise. I guess he'd decided to forget about the night before too. Good. That was easy. We'd just start over. I chatted a few more minutes with them and then Eli leaned over and whispered in my ear. "Let's get out of here, babe. I got something to show you." He waved to Tristan and pulled me into the crowd.

"What, you have a surprise for me?"

"Somethin' like that. You'll see."

I wasn't sure this was a good idea, but I was intrigued to see what the surprise was. A peace offering, most likely? He probably felt bad about the incident at the hotel. And it's not that I had to be afraid of him or anything. Those oozing scabs on his cheek proved I could defend myself, if need be.

He led me to his truck and soon we were driving out of the overcrowded little town. A few miles out he pulled onto a back road I'd never seen before, deeply rutted but cool under broad-spreading branches. We came to a place where a chain across the road blocked our way. A sign hanging from it read "Private Property—Keep Out."

"Well, this is it," Eli said, turning off the engine.

CHAPTER FOURTEEN

"It's on foot from here," Eli said, grabbing his backpack from the bed of his truck.

"Are you sure?" I asked, pointing at the Keep Out sign. "Looks like somebody doesn't want us here."

Eli laughed. "This is the road to your granddaddy's hunting cabin. I don't reckon he'll object."

"Huh. Part of the six hundred acres." My grandfather's land. And someday, now that I thought about it, it would probably be mine and Ryan's. I took the chain that blocked the road in my hand, felt the cool heft of the rusty links. "But you still haven't gotten permission."

"From who?"

"Me," I said. "My grandfather's gone, so you have to ask me now."

Eli rolled his eyes. "May I have your permission to proceed, ma'am?"

"I don't know, you seem like a bad seed. I'm not sure you're the type I want on my property."

"Oh, shut up, you bitch," he said with a snort, stepping over the chain.

Stung by the word, my back stiffened, my head rose, my eyes narrowed. Of course it was a joke, or at least that's what he'd say if I challenged him on his language. But it had a mean undercurrent. It was as if he wanted to psychologically distance himself from me. So much for reconciling, I guess.

And really, there was something strange about this whole field trip. I fingered the bear claw. It was still cool. Even so, I stayed a couple steps behind Eli while we followed the rutted dirt road down a hill. At the bottom a little gray wooden house lay sheltered in a stand of trees.

"Is this it?" I asked, controlling my voice so he wouldn't know I'd been bothered by his offensive comment.

"Not yet."

"But isn't this the hunting cabin?"

"Yeah, but that's not what we're here for," he said. "Nothing to see in there anyways, exceptin' maybe some empty beer cans. We still got a ways to go."

"Let's stop and look inside."

"No!" I was surprised at Eli's vehemence. When he next spoke his voice was softer. "I mean, we want to finish up in time to rehearse later. We don't have time to stop."

After the cabin we no longer followed any recognizable path, but made our way over uneven terrain, rotting leaves thick on the ground and brambles growing in any low place. The trees were dark and densely spaced. Here and there a speckled gray boulder jutted from the ground. Over a little rise, the trees opened up and we stood before a whole pile of boulders, rising from the earth like a jumble of giant gravestones.

Eli considered the pile, eyes darting as if considering something. "This way," he grunted finally, marching in and pulling himself up on top of a big flat rock. He pulled me up after him and we clambered down the other side into a mossy protected area filled with ferns and mushrooms.

He opened his backpack and handed me a flashlight. "You'll want this," he said. He took out a camping lantern for himself.

"For what?"

He laughed. "For the cave. It's pretty dark in there." And with that he squeezed between two boulders into a gap I hadn't noticed before and disappeared, as if he'd dropped down a hole.

"I've never been in a cave before. Is it safe?" I called after him.

His voice came up through the crack. "I been down here dozens a' times. You'll be all right with me. Come on."

I still felt uneasy, but as usual my curiosity pushed aside my good sense and I slipped through after him. *Please don't try anything stupid, Eli. Nothing that would make me have to carve you up again.*

I found myself at the top of a steep slope, with only a little slit of a window in the rocks above to light the way. Eli took my hand and we skidded and slid our way down an unstable mix of soil and pebbles. An occasional wrong-footed step sent cascades of gravel and clouds of dust spewing into the air, the floating particles in sharp relief in the light shafting down from above. We reached the foot of the slope maybe fifty yards down, at a tunnel entrance only big enough for one person to pass through standing up. Cool air, thick with moisture, wafted out from the opening.

Eli switched on his lantern and entered the tunnel. I stayed close behind him. After a couple bends the tunnel become narrower and the ceiling lower, until we were forced to duck while we walked.

"Stop," Eli said. I stopped and we sat down. "Turn out your flashlight." I switched it off and he turned his lantern off. The darkness was total. "We're past the twilight zone," his voice said, slightly echo-ey.

"The twilight zone?"

"It's where the natural light fades out. When you're past it, you're really in the cave."

It was weird, being in complete darkness, and except for some water dripping, complete silence. "So how'd you find this place, anyway?" Though I spoke in a low tone my words seemed loud.

Eli's disembodied voice came from where I knew he was sitting, but with eerie echoes from other directions. "Oh, after Mama died, I did a lot of walkin' in the woods on my own. And one day I found it. In fact, I was led here, you might could say."

I'd never heard him talk about his mother. "How did she die?"

No response for several seconds. "Early," he said finally. Wrong question. I could tell from his tone there wouldn't be any more forthcoming on this topic.

"Huh." I tried to think of something else to say, something that didn't sound so stupid. "You know, it doesn't seem completely dark because I can still see lights in front of my eyes. Flashes, different colors. Like fireworks, almost."

"Yeah, your brain does that. Without the input

from your eyes, it just makes it up." He turned his lantern back on. It was super bright after the absence of light and left me blinking and squinting. "You ready to go now? We'll have to crawl on hands and knees soon."

I turned my own flashlight back on. "Are you serious? You've shown me the cave, I don't need to see any more."

"No, I ain't shown you yet what I wanted you to see. It ain't far now."

I felt a rising fear but dismissed it, rubbing the smoothness of the bear claw between my fingers. We continued, hunched over, down the ever-narrowing passage. Then the ceiling was too low and we crawled along the cold rock floor, hard going with a flashlight in one hand.

"Duck down here," Eli said at one point, dropping to his belly and advancing like a beached walrus.

"What for?"

"A bat's hanging down. Don't touch it or it'll wake up." We belly-crawled underneath the tiny, fuzzy brown bat, hanging curled up in its wings. I shone my flashlight on it to examine more closely.

"No!" Eli hissed. "Put the light down!" I did as he said. "The light'll wake it too."

"So what? He's little. I'm not scared."

"It ain't that," Eli whispered. "You wake him up

and he'll fly out, see the daylight, and come back in. He'll use up his energy without eatin' and might not have enough left to make it out tonight."

"Sorry," I said. "I didn't know bats were so delicate." I glanced back as we left the bat behind. Still hanging, still furry. Kind of cute actually. Gradually I became conscious of the sound of running water in the distance. The burbling became louder the farther we went. Ahead of me, Eli suddenly dropped from sight. What the hell?

"Careful," he called back, his voice coming up from the floor.

I inched forward and looked over the edge into a shaft. Eli was making his way down like a spider, arms and legs spread from wall to wall, his lantern hanging from a belt loop.

He spoke without looking up. "The chimney's only a little ways down and there's plenty of footholds and handholds."

I put my flashlight in my pocket and with quite a bit of trepidation gave it a try myself, though I wasn't able to drop down as smoothly as Eli. I had to turn myself around in the narrow space so I could go down feet first, poking with my foot until I found a place in the rock it fit in. Eli was right, though. It was pretty easy to make my way down, if kind of nerve-wracking, feeling around with a free limb for rocky little ledges and knobs while gripping tight with everything else. At the bottom I stepped through an opening into a huge cavern and shone my flashlight around.

I drew in my breath as I took in the sight. It was beautiful, a natural underground church. The ceiling rose high like in a cathedral, and the stalactites hanging down and stalagmites rising up were the candles, all covered with a coating of white drips, like wax. Some met in the middle to create columns. Water trickled everywhere and the air smelled stoney and moist.

"The cave creek's over this way if you're thirsty," Eli said, picking his way around stalagmites and down an incline to a small stream flowing in a channel. Eli bent down and cupped his hands, bringing the water up to his mouth to drink.

"Is it clean?" I asked.

"Cleaner than anywhere. This here's straight from the source."

I bent over and followed Eli's lead in cupping my hands to bring the water up. It was frigidly cold, but it was the most refreshing water I'd ever tasted, hard and biting and clear as it went down my throat. It must be like the mountain pure water they're always making beer out of in commercials. I drank long, realizing just how dehydrated I was after the hike and the climbing.

When I'd had my fill, Eli was already off, wandering around a grouping of columns to a place where the cavern bulged out, a little apse off the cathedral's main aisle.

"Here," he said as I joined his side. His voice was hushed. "This is what I been aimin' for you to see." He raised the lantern.

The wall was covered with markings. They were like the petroglyphs on the river bluffs, but much more extensive. Little pictures, black lines with red shadings, marching across the walls in neat rows. I stepped close to inspect them. Long-haired men hunting with bows and arrows. Women with babies strapped to their backs kneeling over campfires. And everywhere animals, deer and hawks and wild pigs and panthers and bears and strange, unrecognizable mixes of them.

"This is incredible," I said, my voice barely above a whisper, overcome by the same feeling of an ancient presence I had felt in the canoe.

"And you know what's best, Dani?" Eli said. "I'm the only one who knows this is here. Far as I can tell, I'm the only one who seen it for centuries. I've checked books and not a one has anything like it. Indian art like this just ain't supposed to exist in the Ozarks."

"Is it the same ones who did the drawings on the river?"

"Probably. But those are weathered. Hard to read. These here have been protected by the cave all this time. And come look at this." He stepped into a niche in a wall opposite the drawings. There was a hollowed-out place underneath it and he kneeled down and gazed underneath. I leaned over to see what he was looking at.

"Oh my God!" I said. "There are bones under there!" Hundreds of them, in fact, packed in an area not much bigger than a king-sized bed. A dozen or more large skeletons, and many more small ones, and loose ribs and femurs and fingers and skulls. "Are they human?"

"I reckon some of 'em. Others look like animals. Dogs and birds and things. But I ain't real sure, since I never touched 'em."

I had no intention of touching them myself. "How many times have you been here, anyway?"

Eli rose and took his Razorbacks cap off, ran a hand through his sandy hair. "A lot. I been comin' down here since Mama's passin'."

"How old were you?" I asked, tentatively.

"Eleven."

I was afraid if I said anything more on the subject I'd shut him down again, so I didn't say anything.

Suddenly, my parents' separation didn't seem so bad. At least they were both still around. I felt bad for him, thinking of the loneliness of his house with just him and his dad.

"So," Eli said, hesitating a moment to nervously clear his throat. "I'm gon' need your bear claw."

"My bear claw? What for?" I involuntarily put my hand to my chest.

"For the ritual."

I shook my head. "What are you talking about, Eli?"

"This, Dani, this place." He spread his hands to indicate the drawings, the bones, the columns. "This here's a sacred place, a center of power, a place the Indians chose 'cause spiritual forces can come through here from their world to ours. I know how to do that. But to do it, I need the claw."

I felt the chill of the cave and shivered. The conversation had certainly taken a bizarre and unwelcome turn. My throat tightened. I tried to make sense of Eli's crazy words. A terrible thought entered my brain. "Eli, do you know where my brother is?"

He bit his lower lip and ran a finger around his ear. He knew where he was. He had to know, otherwise he would've answered by now. "Do you know where Ryan is?" I said in a louder tone. My voice echoed shrilly throughout the cavern.

His eyes turned to fierce triangles. "Dani, we got to talk. And we got plenty a' time to do it."

CHAPTER FIFTEEN

Plink. Plink. Plink. Drops of water falling without cease, nature's stalagmite-building leaky faucet. How long between each drop? A couple seconds, it had seemed earlier. Now, a minute. An hour. Maybe whole days were passing in the world above while Eli and I stared at each other down here below.

"Let me explain, all right?" he said finally.

"If you know where Ryan is and you're not telling me, there's nothing to explain."

"Look, I know you hate your brother—"

"I don't hate him. Why would you think that?"

"'Cause you told me, Dani." His voice had taken a pleading tone. "At the Pig, after he massacred your hair. And the way you talk about him. The contempt in your voice. I know you do."

"Huh." I was starting to regret some of the stupid things that had passed through my lips. "I did say that, didn't I?"

"This'll all work out. All we have to do is—"

"Eli, do you know where Ryan is or not?" I made my voice as hard and cold as I could.

"But listen—"

"Do you know where he is?"

Eli sighed and his shoulders slumped. "Yeah." Now we were getting somewhere. "Where?"

"Up at the hunting cabin. I took him out there this mornin'."

I felt muscles all over my body relax at hearing that. I hadn't even realized they were tense before. "Good. Is he okay?"

"Yeah, he came without no problems. It's not like I had to tie him up or somethin'."

"Great. I'll nominate you for a Nobel Peace Prize." I stood up straight. "Let's go get him."

Eli didn't move, his eyes cast down. What was going on in that head of his? Then he grabbed the flashlight from my hands and was off. "Hey!" I cried out, stupidly. I scrambled after him but my foot slipped on the wet rock floor and I tumbled, banging my knee against a protruding stone formation. I exhaled sharply and choked down my instinct to cry out at the tingling pain that went through my leg. I didn't want to give Eli the satisfaction.

"What the hell do you think you're doing?" I screamed after him, pushing myself to my feet. But when I stood pain arced through my knee and my leg collapsed, dropping me in a heap. The lantern light streaked across the cavern, rose in the air, and disappeared. He'd gone up the chimney.

"I'll be back with your brother," his voice echoed. "You wait here." As if I'd be able to go anywhere in the dark. I sat down, back against a column, fuming in the damp, lightless prison. And once I thought Eli was far enough away he wouldn't hear, I screamed, as loud as I could, until my breath was gone.

So there I sat, as good as blind, with the bones and the petroglyphs, the pain in my knee, the fear for Ryan, and the fear for myself, with panic bubbling up in my stomach and my heart beating like I was running a race, and time passed. It seemed like a lot of time, I guess, but it was hard to tell. There was no way to measure it. Nothing to see but black, nothing to feel but cold damp stone, nothing to hear but the endless trickling of water from every direction, an impossibly complicated rhythm of drops in geological surround sound.

It may sound silly, but there was nothing else to do, and no better options, so I prayed. I couldn't pray like Preacher Joab, but I did what I could. I asked God to make sure Ryan was all right, and to help me find a way out of my predicament. And for good measure, I apologized for all the stupid, selfish, short-sighted things I'd done all summer, which took a while.

I didn't know if God heard me, but the praying did seem to soothe my fear. My stomach calmed. I didn't even feel the need to fight panic off. You'd think this would be the time when someone would shriek with terror and fright, left alone in some forgotten place, but I surprised myself with how calm I was.

After a while, I even dozed off a little. Or, I assume I did. I mean, I had a dream. I was searching for Ryan in a forest, only trees and ferns and vines and bushes in every direction, thick and overgrown, and the overwhelming smells of wet soil, pine needles, and lush growing plants. But the intensity of the smells, the solidness of my steps in the soil, the light breeze and all the little sounds of nature gave the dream such clarity and depth, such reality, it seemed less like sleep and more like I had been temporarily transported to a different, actual place.

While I searched, a horrible uneasy feeling clenched my stomach. Where had he disappeared to?

As my anxiety rose, my walk accelerated to a run and then a frantic gallop, wild through the underbrush, ignoring the rough ground and tearing thorns, searching desperately for Ryan and calling out his name. But I had no sense of my direction and no idea where I should look, and I think I just ended up going in circles until I stumbled over a jutting root and crashed through a tangle of vines. I closed my eyes in anticipation of a collision with a tree trunk, but somehow I missed it and landed with a thud on my back.

When I opened my eyes the bottom fell out of my stomach. Before me stood a figure wearing a padded white outfit and a helmet with a plastic faceplate, like an astronaut or a biologist handling dangerous microbes. There must have been a break in the trees because the light was so bright I had to squint when I looked up. Bees buzzed all around the figure, and the glare on the faceplate prevented me from seeing a face.

Indignant, I pushed myself up and rose to my feet. I was certain this person knew where Ryan was and was about to demand the information when the person reached up and removed the helmet. Inside was a man, his face leathery and wrinkled. I blinked a couple times and realized it was Granddad. He still looked the exact same way I remembered from pictures I'd seen of him, years before. White hair. Sharp features, like Aunt Eunice. Red-rimmed rheumy eyes, but clear blue irises fixed on me.

"Granddad?" I asked. He didn't respond. "Granddad, is it you? What are you doing here?"

He put one gloved hand on my shoulder and with the other he took the bear claw between his fingers. "It is good that you wear this," he said.

I nodded, but didn't say anything. I didn't feel like I had to. He smelled nice; a mixture of cologne, mowed grass, and honey. Bees landed on his skin and crawled in his hair, but he didn't brush them away. I felt myself becoming calm as I stood in his presence. I hadn't forgotten Ryan, but somehow my fear that he was in danger passed away. Presently, Granddad leaned over and spoke in my ear. Many times since I've struggled to recall his words, for they had great power and comfort for me, but I've never been able to remember them since.

There I stood, next to my grandfather, not doing anything but breathing in his smell and smiling to be near him and just being…present. After a while it seemed the right time to look for Ryan again. "Can you help me find someone?" I asked him.

"Who are you searching for?" he asked.

"Ryan," I said. "My brother."

"No, not him," Granddad said. "Listen to the bees.

They know. They will tell you where to find the one you search for."

What did that mean? "But I am looking for Ryan," I insisted. "He's missing, and I need to find him."

"He has been here all the time," Granddad said, straightening and pointing his finger. I looked to where he directed my attention. On the other side of the clearing I saw Ryan, hunched over and covered in bees, although strangely he wasn't crying or upset. The insects covered his face, arms, and legs. I ran over and started swatting them off his body and although I was afraid I would be stung, not one harmed me. I wondered why but didn't have time to stop and think about it.

There was a buzzing in my ear. I tried to wave it away, but it persisted. I looked and a bee hovered in mid-air. It was large, almost the size of a hummingbird, yellow and black bands clearly visible. I had the strangest feeling it was... observing us. And then it flew zigzagging off into the trees and in the distance I heard a voice calling. Eli's voice.

———

I sat bolt upright, my dream over instantly. The voice I'd heard hadn't been in my head, it'd been real. Holding my breath in I listened, but there was nothing except the endless dripping. Had hallucinations set in so soon? I would've thought that would take at least a couple days. Unless it had been a couple days? Was that possible?

No, wait. There it was again. Echoing distant voices, too far to hear what they were saying, but clearly recognizable. The higher-pitched one was Ryan, and Eli's deeper voice answering.

CHAPTER SIXTEEN

I angled my head, trying to pick up more of their conversation, but they'd stopped talking. My knee still killed and I was shivering in the damp and chilly cave air. I wrapped my arms around myself, rubbing my hands over the goosebumps on my arms. I wasn't dressed for spending such a long time down here. Then came Eli's and Ryan's voices again, closer now, and the light of Eli's lantern reappeared, descending, on the other side of the cavern. They were coming down the chimney.

"You still down here?" Eli called out. In the distant light I could make out his head, poking out from the chimney entrance.

"Of course I am, you bastard," I yelled back. "Where the hell else would I be?"

"Only makin' sure."

Behind him a smaller figure appeared, holding onto a rope with his hands while he stepped down the wall. So, Eli'd had a rope the whole time. I gritted my teeth so hard I practically chipped a tooth.

The bigger light of the lantern and the smaller light of a flashlight moved across the cave in my direction. As soon as Ryan saw me he ran over and put his arms around me. I hugged him back.

"Dani! I'm so glad you're okay! Eli said you were down here and we had to come help you but he wouldn't tell me what was wrong and I didn't know if you were hurt."

"Okay, slow down! I'm fine." Not true, but I didn't want to worry Ryan about my injured knee at the moment. "What about you? Did he hurt you?"

"Who, Eli? No. He took me to this cabin in the woods and I played X-box 'cause he has like 30 games and he has some Dad doesn't allow me to play even though it kind of stank in the cabin. And I was there all day and I didn't have anything to eat except cold soup in the kitchen. But I didn't even know you were here until just a little while ago when Eli came and got me. And, well, I'm hungry, and now that we found you, can we go now?"

"Yes. I just need to get to my feet." I held my hand out to Ryan and he helped pull me up. I found I was able to stand now although my knee was sore as hell. "Okay, let's get out of here."

"No," Eli said flatly from where he stood. Ryan and I looked at him. His face was underlit by the lantern, like kids do at Halloween to make their faces look spooky. It was working. "Nobody's gon' nowhere 'til we finish up here." He took off his backpack, unzipped it, and dropped it. It hit the ground with a clanking sound. He added, as if making a generous concession, "And after we're done we can go practice for the show tomorrow."

"Screw the show," I said, taking a few limping steps towards the chimney. My heart hurt as I said it, after all that work this summer. *I guess being the second coming of Janis will have to wait. But getting Ryan to safety is a lot more important right now.* I wondered if I'd be able to make it back up, even with the rope.

Eli placed himself in front of me. I stepped around him but he grabbed my arm.

"I said, we ain't finished down here yet." With his free hand, he reached down and pulled something out of the backpack, pointing it at my chest. A hunting knife with a curved metal blade, glinting in the dim light.

"Hey, you let my sister go!" Ryan cried out, running at Eli.

"Ryan, it's fine, stay where you are," I said. He halted. "We'll find out what Eli wants and then we'll leave." I inhaled slowly and deeply to control my breathing, prevent it from becoming ragged. I hoped it all would turn out as well as I'd told Ryan. It struck me that Eli was alternating between domineering and tentative, almost apologetic. Probably a sign he wasn't real sure of what he was doing. Maybe I could take advantage of that.

Eli returned the knife to his backpack and walked us back to the niche with the Indian drawings. "Come an' take a look at this," he said to Ryan.

Ryan glanced at me. "Go ahead," I nodded.

Eli held up the camping lantern to illuminate the various parts of the panorama, explaining each scene in turn. I'd always found Eli's professor act charming before, but at the moment it was seriously grating on my nerves. It wasn't long until Ryan fell under its spell, though, following the pictures along the wall and telling us a story he concocted about a battle between the Indians and the bizarre creatures. At one point, he reached out to touch the wall.

"Hey!" Eli bellowed.

Ryan drew his hand back like he'd burned his finger.

"These are fragile," Eli said. "You can't touch 'em."

"Sorry," Ryan said in a hurt tone. "I didn't know."

"Yeah. Well, I'm sorry for hollerin'," Eli said. "Look at this picture over here, the big 'un. What's it look like to you?"

"Here with the bear?" Ryan answered. "It looks like people fighting. They're killing somebody over at this part, and then over here they're giving the body to a bear, I think."

"That's exactly what they're doin'," Eli said. He put the lantern down and starting taking things out of his pack. Candles. A blanket. A roll of cord. I observed him with suspicion. "You see, the warriors are givin' a gift to the bear. They killed their enemy and now they're presentin' the body to him."

"And then in the next picture this other dead guy is coming to life," Ryan said.

"Exactly. The bear healed their warrior in return for the gift of the dead enemy."

"Cool," Ryan said.

"It is cool, ain't it?" Eli arranged his items on the blanket. "I'm glad you think so. We're gon' be doin' something similar here soon."

Ryan didn't say anything in response, still examining the wall with his flashlight. It was gradually dawning on me what Eli had in mind. But I had to be wrong, because the idea was insane. He couldn't possibly plan to kill Ryan, could he? Maybe I was wrong. Maybe I could draw him out and play on his insecurities at the same time.

"You're crazy, you know that?" I said to him. "I mean literally crazy. These are stories some primitive people drew on a wall. It's not scientific. Whatever you're intending, it won't work."

"You don't think so?" he asked, looking at me with that spooky underlit face. I turned away. "You see these cuts on my face, Ryan?" he asked, pointing to where I'd dug in my fingernails on the hotel roof. "Look like a bear got me, don't it?"

"Yeah," Ryan said. "Did one?"

"Yep. A real she-bear. And she's got the claw to prove it. Don't you, Dani?"

"Batshit insane," was my only response, other than a glare.

"Bet you've even met a bear, ain't you, Dani?"

I didn't say a word. How did he know that?

"I thought so," he said smugly. "You know, it was your bear claw gave you the power to cut me up like this. But I don't hold it against you, Dani. I'm glad it happened that way. It had to. So I'd know that you was the one who was sent to help me." He unwound the roll of cord. "Whether you like it or not."

"What the hell are you droning on about? How am I supposed to help you?"

"The bear, Dani. It can heal. That's why you was sent here. It all makes so much sense. Daddy gettin' sick again, at exactly the same time you come to town." He took a length of cord in each hand. "And you even brought the sacrifice we need." He nodded in Ryan's direction.

My whole body went cold. That confirmed my theory about his intentions, and his insanity. "Sacrifice Ryan?" I said quietly. "To heal your father? You are absolutely off the deep end. Why don't you let the doctors do their job?" Ryan had caught on and was backing away from Eli.

"Doctors don't know shit," Eli spat. "There ain't nothin' more they can do for him. That's what they told him at the hospital. Just like your granddaddy couldn't help my mama."

Ryan kept creeping back but Eli leapt and in instant had him in his arms. I lunged forward but my stupid knee buckled again and I found myself in a prone position on the floor, craning my neck upwards to see what happened. Eli had one arm around Ryan's neck and the other around his body with the cord between his hands. He dragged a twisting, straining Ryan back to the blanket. The hunting knife lay on the blanket's center.

"Let me go, you zombie baby!" Ryan cried. He tried to strike at Eli with a hand he'd worked free but he couldn't reach around far enough.

Not knowing what else to do, I reached into my

shirt for the bear claw. Cold. Inert. Lot of good it was doing me now. Just because it wasn't me personally in danger it had decided to take a break. I forced myself to my feet. Eli had dragged Ryan to the blanket and was trying to loop the cord around him.

Ryan reached in his jeans pocket with his free hand. What was he doing? When he pulled his hand back out there was something in it. He jammed his hand back and caught Eli in the thigh.

"Son of a bitch!" Eli yelled, stumbling back and letting Ryan slip free. "What the hell did you do to me?" A wet red stain swelled across Eli's pant leg. Whatever Ryan had stabbed him with was still embedded. Eli leaned over and pulled it out with a grunt.

Meanwhile, I had limped my way to the blanket and picked up the hunting knife. I took a step towards Eli. "Get out of here, now," I said to him in a low voice, waving the knife. I gritted my teeth so he wouldn't see how much pain my knee was putting me in.

He looked up from his wounded thigh, sneering. "What you gon' do, Dani? Stab me? I don't think so." He returned his attention to stanching the flow of his blood.

Maybe he was right. Even if I had been in condition to, was I really the kind of person who could attack another with a knife? That was his department, not mine. But then I thought of Ryan, and what Eli might do to him if I didn't stop him. And I knew I could do it if I had to. Stab Eli. Kill him. But I also knew from Eli's own wavering performance that he wasn't nearly as confident as he was making himself look. And I had an idea I could avoid the whole situation if I put on a show.

"You're right, I couldn't stab you. But I feel the bear in me," I said, giving my voice a hoarse whisper I hoped sounded badass. He rose to a standing position with a half-smirk on his face. I kept going. "She can do what I can't do. Just like before, on top of the hotel. She's getting stronger. I'm trying to hold her down, but she wants to come out." I lifted my voice, tried to give it a touch of hysteria. "She's coming out, Eli. She wants a victim here tonight, like you planned. A sacrifice. Only it's you she wants to take." All the time I was talking I advanced toward him, ignoring my knee and gripping the knife handle as if I had some idea what I was doing with it.

Eli's smirk had disappeared and his eyes darted around. He seemed doubtful. I took another step and actually, now that I'd given the big speech, I did feel something welling up in me, something strong and hungry and merciless. I made a bear growl in my throat, and was surprised at how ferocious it came out. Eli glanced at me and his face turned a little pale when he saw my eyes. He took a step back, then another. My arms felt mighty, and when I breathed in I could actually smell the fear coming out in Eli's sweat, a kind of thin musk rising in the air off his skin. "Go," I yelled, and the word burst from my throat in a roar, resounding through the cavern.

Eli went. He stumbled backwards, picked himself up and kept going, maintaining his eyes on me all the while. When he passed the camping lantern he picked it up. I kept advancing. He turned and broke into a run and made it to the chimney, climbing up with haste. "Ryan, get over there," I shouted. "Before he can pull up the rope!" Ryan was patting around on the ground near the blanket, searching for something. "Hurry!"

"I can't go without my flashlight! I dropped it around here!" He kept patting as if that was the most important thing, while the lantern light receded. No time to wait for him so I hobbled over to the chimney, but by the time I got there Eli was at the top pulling the rope after him.

"You bastard!" I screamed after him, but he didn't respond.

Ryan joined me at my side. "I found it," he said, swinging the flashlight beam around.

"Good job," I said, sighing. No use getting angry,

it was too late to make a difference. Too bad, though, because there was no way I could make it up with my knee, and Ryan was too little to spider crawl up.

"You know, you looked really scary there for a minute," Ryan said.

I smiled. "I felt a little scary. What was it you stabbed him with, anyway?"

"One of the Indian spear points Dad gave me."

"Of course, the spear points," I said, nodding. Twisted as his thinking was, Eli had been right about one thing. All the events of the summer did seem to fit together, in a strange way.

"Dani, it's really dark in here," Ryan said. He held out his hand and I took it.

"I know," I said. "We'll find our way out."

"What if we can't? Do you think anybody will find us?"

"Sure," I said, though I wasn't. "They're probably looking for us already. Even before I came down here Dad was worried about where you were."

"Oh," he said. He seemed unconvinced. "Why did Eli do all that?"

"I don't know, Ryan. I don't know."

We made our way around the edge of the cavern, shining the flashlight in every crevice, searching for some possible way back to the surface other than the chimney. The place was pretty big, and it was tough going in some parts, scrambling over rubble piles or squeezing through narrow archways. My knee slowed us down, failing painfully whenever I managed to twist it just right, which was often. We'd just about circled the whole cavern when the flashlight flickered and dimmed slightly. I didn't say anything, hoping Ryan hadn't noticed. No such luck.

"The flashlight, Dani. If it goes out, we'll be completely in the dark." His eyes were large and fearful, and his grip on my hand tightened.

I breathed in slowly. A nagging anxious lump swelled up in my stomach, but I forced it down. I had to remain calm, for his sake. "Let's turn it off to conserve the battery. We'll sit right over here. We can take a little nap. And when we wake up, we can turn it on again."

"Okay. But I'm thirsty. I need a drink first."

We crossed to the creek. Ryan leaned over and drank and I aimlessly ambled a few steps along the edge. And then, I noticed the bear claw got warm. I took a few more steps. Warmer still.

"Hey, where are you going with the light?" Ryan called after me.

"I'm just testing something."

"What are you testing? What is it? Is something there?"

"Just be quiet a minute." With each step the bear

claw heated up more. The creek ended in a little pool at one end of the cavern. I swept the flashlight across the water and saw that it flowed under a sort of natural archway.

I pondered whether I should wade in to examine further. My jeans would be wet but I didn't really have much other choice. I stepped in. The water was so frigid it numbed my feet and calves in seconds and set my hurt knee to throbbing. But at the same time, the bear claw grew so hot I had to hold the chain out from my skin. I stepped back onto dry rock, my jeans dripping and shoes sloshing.

"What's wrong? Why are you holding out your necklace like that?" Ryan had made his way to the edge of the pool.

"It's burning hot," I said.

"Let me feel it." He touched his finger against the claw. "Yeah, you're right. Why is your necklace hot?"

"I think maybe it's trying to tell me something."

"What?" Ryan asked. "What's it trying to tell you?"

I shone the visibly weakening flashlight beam under the arch. There did seem to be an opening under it. Was it a passage, or was the refraction of the light playing a trick on my eyes? I stepped in the water again, strode right up to the arch, icy water up to my thighs now and flowing with some force. Bear claw searing hot. Yep, it was a tunnel underneath, all right. Looked broad enough to swim in. But where did it go? Should we try to swim through?

I heard a splash and then Ryan was standing next to me, the water up to his waist.

"The water's so cold," he said. He reached out and touched the bear claw. "Ow! It's hotter than before."

"I think it wants us to swim into that tunnel."

"I don't want to go in water this cold, Dani. It hurts. And what if the tunnel doesn't come out somewhere with air?"

"I don't know." Strange that Ryan was the voice of reason now. I shook my head. Obviously swimming for it was insanely dangerous.

"I can hold my breath for 54 seconds," he said.

"That's pretty good," I said. And then the flashlight flickered and died. We stood in the freezing cold water in the absolutely dark cave and neither of us said a word.

CHAPTER SEVENTEEN

I shook the flashlight, clicked it on and off. No response. In disgust I screamed and threw it as far into the cave as I could. There was a clattering jangle of parts when it landed. And then, with nothing else to do, I stood there with the freezing water swirling past my legs, stupidly holding the burning hot bear claw away from my skin.

After a minute I heard a sound above the burbling that sounded like somebody lightly drumming, as if with chopsticks. It was Ryan's teeth chattering. My stomach tightened because in a way, it was my fault he was here in the cold, wet, and complete dark. If I hadn't been so overdramatic over the hair incident and convinced Eli I hated him all this might never have happened. And now we were probably going to die here.

"D-Dani," Ryan said, "Is s-something glowing in the water?"

"What?" I said, looking around and not seeing anything.

"In the t-tunnel. It l-looks like something's glowing."

I gazed into the tunnel. He was right. It was just possible to make out a faint amber glimmer far off in the water. I drew in my breath. Could it be daylight? The bear claw was practically ready to burst into flames.

"54 seconds, huh?" I said.

"Y-yeah. But th-that was two weeks ago. I m-might be able to hold it a whole m-minute now."

Think it through, Dani. Obviously, swimming for it was a terrible idea. But so was staying in the cave in our wet clothes until hypothermia set in, and I bet that wouldn't take long. We were going to die either way. Fast or slow? Better to die taking a chance than freezing to death in some cave of horrors. *Screw it. Let's go. Now, before I think about it too much and lose my nerve.* I found Ryan's hand in the dark and squeezed it. "We can do this. Ready?"

"Y-y-yeah."

"On the count of three we'll do it. Straight toward the light. One. Two. Three." We plunged into the water. Oh God, it was cold, so cold it cut straight through to my bones. For a second I didn't move, simply floated. One part of my brain knew I should swim but another part had decided it simply wasn't worth it.

The water stirred beside me, little eddies swirling across my skin from Ryan's strokes. The sensation roused me from my momentary shock and I kicked my legs, moving into the tunnel. It was hard swimming in blue jeans but the current was on our side, pushing us through. The clear, cold water grew brighter as we swam closer to the glow. Up ahead the tunnel opened up, the glow suffusing the water from above the surface. Slowly I breathed out, releasing a stream of bubbles. It was so cold and I wanted to go up for air, but we weren't there yet. Almost.

I had a moment of panic when I turned my head and saw Ryan already swimming to the top. Not yet, Ryan, we're so close but not yet. I reached up and pulled his pant leg. He moved down a little. Now my lungs were really aching. So close to the end of the tunnel. Only a few more strokes, if I can just keep from breathing in, if I can just force my heavy limbs to keep going, and then I was there in the pastel yellow light, and Ryan too, and we burst to the surface at the same time and sucked in huge lungfuls of air.

We found ourselves in a pool under a rocky overhang with trees growing in the soil around the edge. The sky was pale with early morning sunlight. Trees and sky. Pine needles and fresh air.

"We m-made it," Ryan said. I was too out of breath to answer but I took his hand in mine.

We swam to the shore and climbed out. The pool emptied into a little creek and without speaking we followed along its edge, having no real idea where to go. I think we both sensed that walking was the best way to keep warm. I myself was shivering in my wet clothes but when I looked over at Ryan he was shaking uncontrollably and his cheeks and lips were whitish-blue. Not a good sign. We walked for several minutes, which warmed us up a little. At least it took the edge off. And then we heard distant voices. We looked at each other.

"Over here!" we shouted. "Help!"

"Dani! Ryan! Is that you?" came a man's voice back.

"Yes! Over here!" The sound of someone crashing through underbrush, footsteps, and then Austin and Preacher Joab were running towards us from out of the trees.

"Oh, God, thank the Lord above you two are safe. Are y'all okay?" Joab asked as he rushed up. He reached out and embraced us both, holding us close against him with his beefy arms. I remembered my earlier judgment of him as buffoonish and insincere and felt ashamed.

"Fine," I said. "We're fine, mostly. But we're dripping on you."

"We're c-cold," Ryan said.

"Son, you are positively blue," Joab said, letting us go and looking Ryan over. "And here I am jawin' away. Austin, we need to get these two into our dry clothes."

"Yes, sir." Austin already had his t-shirt and jeans off before Joab had even made the suggestion, and his father followed suit with his polo shirt and khakis. Austin looked at me with his brown doe eyes. "We been lookin' for y'all all night," he said, peeling Ryan's clothes off and helping him into his own dry ones. "A lot of folks out lookin' for y'all, actually."

"We prayed to the Lord that we would find you, and He led us right here," Joab said, handing me his garments. "I'll just turn around now and you get yourself right into these, Miss Moser. I apologize for my flabbiness, but I don't figger you mind right about now."

"Not at all," I said. "Thank you for lending them to us." I smiled to see Austin averting his eyes from me while I undressed, even as he was still helping Ryan.

"What do you think, missie?" Joab asked, his back towards me. "Can we Praise the Lord we found you safe and whole?"

"You know, I was kind of thinking for a while there the Lord had forgotten about Ryan and me," I said.

"A father never forgets his children, Dani. Don't you never forget that. Ain't that right, Austin?"

"Yes, sir." Austin had finished with Ryan and gave his shoulder a squeeze. "Clothes are a little big on you. But at least they're dry." Ryan had stopped shivering and a little color was returning to his face.

"Now what about Eli?" Joab said. "Wasn't he with y'all?"

"Eli's not with us," I said, practically spitting his name out. "It's his fault we were down there in the first place. And no, I don't know where he is."

"Well, let's walk on up to your Aunt's house and let folks know you been found so they kin stop worryin'," Joab said.

"Aunt Eunice's house? Are we close to it?"

"Not too far," Austin said.

I looked around, and there, right in front of us, was the thong tree we'd seen on the hike with Aunt Eunice. It dawned on me: it was pointing at the creek because the creek led to the cave entrance. That was the significant spot the Indians were marking. How many centuries had it been since anyone had used their secret entrance until Ryan and I found it?

I breathed deeply. The crisp outside air felt good in my chest after all that time breathing in the cave dampness. We started up the path to Springbloom.

I don't think I've ever been so glad to get to a place as Aunt Eunice's warm kitchen that morning. While Preacher Joab called my dad, the sheriff's office, and everybody else out hunting for us to tell them we'd been found, Aunt Eunice got to work cooking, using Austin to run little errands for her while Ryan and I sat cozy under blankets.

She soon had heaping plates for us, loaded with biscuits and oyster mushroom gravy and mushroom omelets. Ryan and I were ravenous, having not eaten since lunchtime the day before. Soon she seated Joab and Austin at the table with plates of their own.

"Now I want y'all to tell me exactly what happened," Aunt Eunice said, taking her own seat. "I'm sure y'all will have to tell the story a hundred times today, so you might as well get used to explaining it."

Ryan and I related the events of the previous twenty- four hours, each contributing what we knew, although I left out all the parts about the bear claw and I guess Ryan was too shaken up to notice the oversight. Our story was crazy enough already, and I didn't want to push it past the point of plausibility. When we had finished, she shook her head and remarked, "That poor boy. That poor, poor boy."

"Who, Aunt Eunice?" Ryan asked. "I feel fine now."

"I'm speaking of Eli, dear."

"What for?" I asked. "Didn't I just tell you he nearly succeeded in killing us?"

Joab put his hands on the table and sighed. "Dani, Enos went back to the hospital yesterday morning. He's in critical condition. This could be the end." My stomach fell. "When somebody called in seein' Eli's truck at the top of the road to the hunting cabin, and then nobody could find y'all…"

"His state of mind in no way excuses what he did to you and Ryan," Aunt Eunice said. She put her hand on my shoulder and squeezed it. "But I cannot even imagine how confused that boy's head must be right now."

All the routes to and from Adelaide were full of traffic for the folk festival. It was strange seeing so many cars on those little twisty roads. It took about twice as long as usual to get back into town, just when I was so impatient to get back.

When we pulled in front of the rental house, Dad didn't even wait for Aunt Eunice to turn the engine off before he had the passenger door open and Ryan and me in his arms. "Oh, thank God you two are safe," he said. "Oh, God, I was so worried." We hugged him back and when I looked at his face, he had tears running down his cheeks he didn't even bother brushing away.

It wasn't long before Ryan and Dad and me were inside at the kitchen table while I explained the story for the second time. Again, I left out the part about the bear claw. And when we were done, Dad and Aunt Eunice looked at each other.

"What do you think, Jim?" she asked, her eyebrows raised.

"I think it's remarkable," Dad said. "I'm proud of both of you. You were very brave. But...."

He stopped, as if he were about to say something else but decided against it. Coffee dripped in the coffee- maker on the counter. Muffled shouts and loud laughs came from the crowd at the festival.

"But what?" I said.

"But I do have some questions." He tapped the table a couple times. "You see, it sounds to your Aunt and me like you two are leaving some parts out."

PART FOUR: DOWN ON ME

CHAPTER EIGHTEEN

Ryan and I sat speechless while Dad and Aunt Eunice
regarded us with poker faces. I couldn't decide
whether I was more shocked that Dad had called me
out on lying, or that he and Aunt Eunice clearly
knew more about the situation than I'd assumed.

"I'm sorry?" I said finally. "What do you think
we're leaving out?"

"You tell me," Dad said. "Maybe start with that
bear claw on your necklace."

I didn't respond. Wasn't quite sure how to,
actually. Aunt Eunice reached up and tapped the
feather in her hair. "Your daddy and I have been
down in that cave too," she said gently. "And we've
had more experience than you might think with
what's down there."

She pulled the feather out and passed it to Ryan and me to examine. The quill was thick and nearly a foot long, the barbs black along one side and metallic blue on the other. "Now what kind of bird do y'all reckon this is from?" she asked us when we handed it back.

"A big one," Ryan said.

"Certainly," Aunt Eunice said. "What do you think, Dani?"

"I don't know. A blue heron, maybe?"

Aunt Eunice smiled. "Good girl. You've picked something up living with me this summer. A great blue heron. I wear this feather in my hair always. Even at night I keep it right by my bed. And where do you think I got this feather, Ryan?"

"Did you find it behind your house?" he guessed.

"No, dear. I received it from the heron himself."

"How did he do that?" I asked, leaning forward to hear better.

"Why, I met him at the edge of a fishing pond, early one morning long ago. He stood there on one leg and told me to step up to him and pluck it from his wing. And I've carried it ever since." She slid the feather back in her hair. From outside we could hear distant voices as the folk festival crowd gathered.

"Is that true, Aunt Eunice?" Ryan asked.

"Every word, dear. And do you know what this

feather has done for me since I started wearing it?"

"What?" Ryan's eyes were large with curiosity.

"Well, it's done this," she said, clearing her throat. "At a time in my life when I was wild, it brought me dignity. Later on I found myself without companionship for the first time in many years, and it taught me how to live alone without feeling lonely. And sometimes, when those I love are in trouble—" and here she looked me in the eye—"it offers me guidance for helping them." She gestured to Ryan and me. "Sound anything like the story with that bear claw?"

"A little." I removed the necklace, setting it on the kitchen table. Clearly it was time to fill Dad and Aunt Eunice in on the bear. "I wasn't trying to lie, you know. Only the part of the story with the claw sounded so unbelievable. I'm not sure I believe it myself."

"We understand, Dani," Dad said. "Go ahead and tell us."

"This bear claw definitely saved our lives," I said. "But it might be easier if I started from the beginning." Dad and Aunt Eunice nodded, so I went all the way back and explained everything: the dream about the bear at the scenic lookout, the night I met the bear in the woods and it had breathed into me, how the claw had guided Ryan and me out of the cave. Ryan added in a few details of his own from the night before. And finally, though at first I intended to leave it out, once I got going I couldn't help but tell how the claw had helped me defend myself against Eli on the roof of the hotel.

Dad and Aunt Eunice looked grim when they heard how he had attacked me. "Well, at least, I don't suppose he'll try that with you again." Dad gave a tight-lipped smile.

"No, I don't think he will," I said. It was quiet for a minute.

Ryan rubbed his eyes and yawned. He looked so small and vulnerable in the kitchen chair that was too big for him. A feeling of protectiveness came over me. I regretted so much all the mean things I'd thought and said about him lately. It hadn't always been like this. When we were younger we'd been friends, inseparable at times. I'd taught him how to play checkers, dressed him up in costumes, included him in games with the neighborhood kids. What had happened? I determined on the spot I'd try to bring that old relationship back. Ryan was one of the bravest kids I knew, and I wouldn't want anybody else for a brother.

"You've had a long night, young man," Dad said. "Let's say we get you in bed."

Ryan protested a little, but it was more for show

than out of conviction, and Dad soon had him back in his room. Aunt Eunice rose and made tea while we waited, mixing sumac berries, cloves, and cinnamon in a saucepan of water on the stove. When the water came to a boil, she removed it and strained the hot water through a sieve lined with cheesecloth. She let it cool for a couple minutes and brought me a cup, still steaming and clear with a hint of pink, and when I sipped some it puckered my lips with its tanginess.

Dad rejoined us in the kitchen. "His eyes were closed before his head even hit the pillow," he said, standing behind me, running his fingers along the side of my face and through my hair. "You'll probably want to hit the hay soon, too, I imagine." I leaned my head back. I couldn't remember him doing that since I was a little girl, unable to sleep until Daddy came and stroked my head. I groaned inwardly when the phone rang, interrupting the moment.

Dad answered it. "Hello? Yes it is…No, we haven't seen him." He gave me a glance and took the phone into the other room, closing the kitchen door behind him. I heard his muffled voice but couldn't make out the words. He spoke for only a couple minute and came back in with a somber face. "That was a sheriff's deputy," he said. "Seems Eli was spotted about a half hour ago by some out-of-town visitors."

"Was he all right?" Aunt Eunice asked.

"No, that's why they called it in. His pants were bloody and he was behaving erratically, talking to himself and waving his hands. When they approached him, he cursed them out."

"Where was it?" I asked.

"Parking lot of the old motel," Dad said. "But a deputy went there to check and he was nowhere to be found. That's why they called us, to see if we had an idea where he might be. I guess they're afraid he might be suicidal, or ready to hurt somebody."

That settled it. A resolution had been forming itself in my mind all morning, but in that instant, I was certain.

I put my mug down and stood. "I've got to go and find him."

CHAPTER NINETEEN

"You've got to do what?" Dad said, his voice rising with disbelief. Aunt Eunice raised her eyebrows.

"To find Eli," I said. "I have to do it, before something happens."

"Something like him seriously hurting you," Dad said, his face flushing. "The way he's tried to hurt you twice already. No, absolutely not. I've already lost you once in the past twenty-four hours, I don't want it to happen again."

I set my jaw and prepared to argue. I had it all pictured perfectly in my head. One final confrontation with Eli. Give him a piece of my mind. Or save him from himself. I wasn't sure which yet.

I looked at Dad, standing there, forehead furrowed and fists half-clenched. I had to make my case to him, but not with a fight. That wouldn't get me anywhere. A mature appeal, calm discussion. Put forward my best reasons and hear what he had to say. After all, he was right, from his point of view. It would be dangerous and stupid of me to look for Eli. I really should go to bed like Ryan. I had to show him that these were extenuating circumstances.

"Dad, I won't argue," I said, keeping my voice even. "If you want me to stay here, I will. But I feel like my whole reason for being here this summer is connected to Eli. Living through last night was only half my task. That's why the bear breathed into me the other night. To give me strength to see this through to the end. I might be the only one who can find Eli, and it's my responsibility."

"It's not your responsibility," he said firmly. "It's the sheriff's. Your job is to get some sleep after your ordeal."

I took a deep breath and continued. "Then why are we here?" I asked. "That's something I haven't understood since June. Settling Granddad's estate only took a week. But we're here the whole summer. Why did we stay? Why did you bring Ryan and me here for this whole time?"

Dad stammered a little with his answer. "Well, I've been trying to find a buyer for the old place. And we needed to get back on our feet after a rough year." He hesitated before going on. "And your mom and I needed a break from each other, a little time off. I thought we all needed to get away and decompress for a while, and it felt like this was the place to do it."

There was my opening. This was how I could show him. "Dad, that feeling you had is the feeling I have now," I said. "This is how *I* can get back on *my* feet. This is how I can fulfill my purpose here."

Aunt Eunice put down her mug on the counter and nudged Dad. "You know, Jim," she said quietly, "if Austin went with her, she'd have someone to protect her. Between him and the bear claw, they should be able to handle Eli, whatever state he's in." I had to admit it, Aunt Eunice was good. She knew Dad liked Austin.

Dad sighed. "You two are going to break me down in the end, aren't you? Okay, you and Austin can go, and I'll follow you in my car."

I shook my head. "Won't work. As soon as Eli sees you he'll head in the other direction. Only I can do this. It's something I need to do."

"I should have my sanity checked," Dad said, shaking his head. "Fine. You and Austin. But be careful. Austin needs to be with you the whole time. And listen, you call me every hour to check in. If you get in any trouble you can't handle, or even suspect you can't handle, you call me. Do you understand me, Danielle?"

"I do. I will."

"Good. See that you do." He hugged me and held me close for a long time.

The first place Austin and I hit was Eli's house. We cleared the festival traffic around town and were out on the back roads in a few minutes. It was a beautiful morning and we drove with the windows down, the late summer sun gentler and milder than it had been in weeks and the fragrances of the woods swirling around us like a bath.

When we got there Austin checked the outside and I took the inside. The house felt empty before I even opened the door. It was unlocked and I knew I wouldn't find anything, but I went through the place anyway. Dirty dishes in the sink, a couple full ashtrays, but no sign anybody'd been there for a while. In Eli's room books were strewn across the floor. One was open, face-down, next to his bed. *Native American Beliefs and Blood Rituals.*

Eli's white Persian followed me, meowing and rubbing against my legs whenever I stopped. How long had it been since she'd been fed? At least a day, possibly longer. In the pantry I found a bag of cat food, put some in a bowl and set it out on the front stoop. "Here you go, Iloka," I said. She forgot all about me and turned to the bowl hungrily. I pulled the front door closed behind me.

"Anything?" asked Austin, coming around the side of the house.

"No," I said. "But I didn't think there would be."

"Still had to make sure," he said. We got in the truck and Austin hit the gas on the way back to town, but it wasn't long until the roads were crowded with out- of-state plates and we slowed to pedestrian speed. He turned off on the bypass that went by Aunt Eunice's.

"But this is the long way around," I said.

"Better'n sittin' in that traffic jam. All those cars, probably take us the same time to get there anyways." He gunned the engine and got us back up to highway speed.

"Thanks for helping me," I said. He nodded once. "I really mean it. I know you and Eli aren't exactly best friends."

"Not so much," he said.

"But Shea told me you used to be." I studied his face to see his reaction.

He kept his eyes on the road, impassive except the corner of one lip turning down. "Shea, huh? It figgers." He tapped his fingers on the steering wheel. "Yep. We knew each other up from kindergarten. We even used to play together."

"That's funny to think," I said. "You and him, sharing your toys."

"No, I mean we really played together." Austin took his hands off the steering wheel to mimic playing a violin. "At the Cultural Center. Me and Daddy on fiddle, he and his mama on guitar."

"Really? In front of people and everything?" I asked. I hadn't even realized he played the fiddle. Austin nodded. "How old were you?"

"First time, probably 'bout age six," he said.

Geez, they'd known each other forever. I wondered if Adelaide made up for being such a small town by the complication and depth of its relationships. Not as many people, but every person here had a long history with everybody else. Fewer leaves on the tree, but deeper roots. "So what happened to you two?" I asked.

A car unexpectedly cut in front of us from out of a driveway and we came to a jolting stop. "Look where you're goin', you damn fool!" Austin yelled out the window. "You okay?"

"Yeah, I'm fine."

"Sorry about the cussin'." He didn't say anything for a while after that. Maybe he'd forgotten my question, or more likely, was deflecting it. But then he spoke. "Eli changed after his mama died. I don't know why."

"How did he change?" I asked gently.

"Hard to get along with. Started hanging out with Corey and that crowd." He hesitated. "Don't get me wrong. Ain't nothin' wrong with Corey 'n' them. But they're into gettin' drunk, gettin' high, all that. Don't interest me." His hand gripped the wheel. "I reckon you think I'm old-fashioned."

I smiled. I couldn't believe how much Austin was actually opening up to me now. "I'm appreciating the old-fashionedness a lot more today than yesterday."

Austin went on. "About a year ago he started coming to church. Daddy was so happy to see it. What do you reckon the cause was?"

I shook my head. "I can't imagine." It was tough to picture Eli going to Joab's church willingly.

"A girl."

"Ah, of course," I said.

"Real pretty," Austin said. "Shy. Becca, her name was. Her family'd come up from Creekboro to attend services. She come to our house all in tears one night. Seems Eli got her pregnant." He breathed in deeply. "He knocked her up and didn't want nothin' to do with her when she told him. She was scared to tell her own folks."

"Oh my God." I stared at the road ahead in disbelief. "What happened?"

"I went over to Eli's house, try and convince him to be a man. Do the honorable thing. Got nothin' but an earful of cussin' for my trouble. That's when things between me and Eli became downright hostile."

"What about Becca?"

He shrugged. "Don't know. Her family stopped comin' to church. She never answered when Daddy or me called."

"Did she have the baby?"

"I reckon so," he said. Just then we passed by Springbloom. Through a gap in the trees I could see cop cars out front. Probably something to do with my disappearance, maybe some paperwork. Still, something about them gave me a bad feeling.

"Stop the truck," I said.

"What? Why?"

"Just stop it and drive back to Eunice's." He turned the truck around. At the end of the gravel driveway two sheriff's cars gleamed white in the sun. We pushed open the screen door and found Aunt Eunice at the kitchen sink, ferociously scrubbing a pan and sending little splashes of soapy water everywhere. I heard Ruskin barking somewhere in the house, but it sounded muffled, and strange noises came from the upper level.

"Howdy," she said to us. "How're y'all kids

doing?"

"We're fine," I said. "Long time no see."

Aunt Eunice nodded with a vague smile. Something seemed off. Maybe it was the way she attacked a baking sheet with a scrub brush like getting it clean was a matter of life and death. "Is everything here okay?"

"Well, I'm sure glad to see you," she said. "You kids must be hungry. Sit down and I'll fix you something."

We took our chairs. The muffled barking grew more insistent. "Where's Ruskin? Is he trapped in a closet somewhere?" I asked.

"Oh, I had to put him away while the guests are here," Aunt Eunice said.

"You mean the sheriff? I saw the cars outside."

Two sheriff's deputies entered the kitchen even as I asked the question. "We're done with the search, ma'am," one of them said.

"Well, did you find what you were looking for?" she asked.

"We found some suspicious plants outside, if that's what you mean," the deputy said. "We're going to have to take you in."

"Does that mean I'm under arrest?" Aunt Eunice asked him.

"Yes, ma'am, I'm afraid so." His radio crackled.

"What's he talking about? Arrest you?" I said, standing up so fast my chair fell back behind me, hitting the floor with a thunk. The two deputies ignored me completely.

"Please hold your hands out, Mrs. Packard." She did so and one of the deputies locked a pair of handcuffs around her wrists. It was strange to hear somebody call her by her last name.

"What were they talking about, Aunt Eunice? Why would you be under arrest?" My stomach dropped out and my mind spun as I tried to comprehend. An hour before I'd been sitting at the kitchen table with her, now she was being taken to jail. I felt Austin's hand on my shoulder.

Aunt Eunice's voice was artificially cheery. She was putting on a show for us. "Oh, it seems while they were tramping around last night, one of the deputies came across a patch of marijuana growing out on my land," she said.

"But…that's terrible!" I said. Still, now I felt a little relief, knowing at least this would be cleared up soon. Clearly Aunt Eunice didn't have anything to do with it. "Who would plant that on your property?"

"Why, I would, Dani," she said. "It belonged to me."

The feeling of relief collapsed, or maybe that was just my jaw. "Please step out of the way, ma'am," a deputy said to me, escorting Aunt Eunice outside.

Out on the porch, Aunt Eunice stopped the deputy and called back through the screen door. "Go let Ruskin out of the laundry room. And if I'm not back tonight, come by and feed him, would you?"

"I will," I said, bewildered. This was all happening so fast. I had no clue how to react so I just stood there with my mouth open.

"Don't you worry about me, Dani. You and Austin go find Eli. He's the one who really needs your help." The deputy took her by the arm and led her down the porch steps.

CHAPTER TWENTY

The drive back to town was awfully quiet. The house had been a mess. Every drawer pulled open and emptied, clothes on the floor, furniture overturned. Of course they'd gone through my stuff too. I can't explain how angry I was when I'd discovered my guitar out of its case and leaned precariously against a wall. Thank God it wasn't damaged. Of course, this was all my fault, at root. If I hadn't been so stupid about Ryan and the hair incident, the whole chain of events leading up to this wouldn't have happened. Anger and guilt mixed in my gut like I'd swallowed gasoline.

I didn't even ask Austin where we were headed next, but he seemed to have a destination in mind. I wasn't too surprised when we ended up walking down the familiar steps to Tristan's basement apartment.

Tristan opened his door wearing a black form-fitting t-shirt and cut-off jean shorts, a cigarette in his mouth and a roll of packing tape in one hand. "Oh, it's you two. Come on in." Inside the basement apartment there were moving boxes, a suitcase open on the bed, his instrument cases by the door. "Man, you two look glum," he said. "Somebody's dog die?"

"Don't ask," I said. "You going somewhere?"

"Yeah, end of the summer. Gotta get back to Fayetteville tomorrow." I remembered Fayetteville was the home of the University of Arkansas.

"Really? You're in school?"

"Yeah. As much as I love working down at the gravel plant, it's not how I want to spend my whole life, you know." He put the roll of tape on the windowsill and picked up a stack of paperbacks on his bed, finding an open space for them in one of the boxes.

"Hey, Tristan," I said. "Don't take this the wrong way, but…"

"Yeesss?" He looked at me with raised eyebrows.

"Aren't you a little old to be going to college?"

He laughed. "Probably. I took some time off to travel. Chile. Bolivia. Chiapas. Oaxaca. Guatemala."

How many times had I rehearsed with Tristan this

summer? Fifteen? Twenty? Why did I know so little about this guy? "Wow, that's really cool," I said.

He put his cigarette out in an ashtray on his dresser. "I highly recommend the same course of action for you too, little bird. Take a few years and see where your guitar leads you."

"Well, I'll probably need to get a job."

"Just enough to pay the bills, though. Nothin' you can't pick up and leave whenever you get the urge. You'll have your whole life to be in sales or accounting or a corporate lawyer or whatever. See what it's like to really live first."

Austin cleared his throat.

"Oh, right," I said. "Look, have you seen Eli?"

"You mean since yesterday? No. I thought he went somewhere with you."

"Yeah, that didn't turn out so well. But his dad's in the hospital and nobody's seen him."

"Hmm." Tristan mused a minute. "That's no good. I wonder if he'll show up tonight?"

"'Tonight?" I asked. "Why then?"

"For our show? Remember?"

Oh, right. The show that twenty-four hours ago had seemed like the most important thing in the world. So much for that. "Are you kidding?" I said. "Did you hear what I said about his dad?"

"It'll be tough to play without him." He stuffed a

stack of underwear into a corner of his suitcase. He seemed pretty nonchalant about the whole thing.

"So, you didn't hear that we were... missing or anything? Eli and my brother and me?"

"No," Tristan said. "Were you?"

"Yes! Everybody was looking for us. The sheriff and everything."

Tristan whistled. "Wow, sorry to hear that. When you and Eli didn't show up to rehearse last night I dropped some acid. I've been kind of out of it, you know? So where were you missing?"

A nudge from Austin. "Never mind that," I said, sighing. "Where do you think Eli might be?"

Tristan pushed his suitcase aside so he could sit on the edge of the bed. He closed his eyes and rubbed above his temple. The movement made the tattoos on his arms dance in the dim light. "Huh. Eli's a real private person. As long as I've known him, he deals with issues by disappearing." He kept rubbing his head for several moments, like a mentalist pulling the answer out of the air. His eyes snapped open. "Got it. You checked the Piggly Wiggly?"

"Uh, no. You think he'd go to work when he wanted to disappear?"

"Last place you'd think to look, right?" Austin and I looked at each other. Actually, Tristan's point was logical, sort of.

"Okay, we'll try the Pig," I said. It's not like we had any other leads at this point. Austin already had the door open and one foot out. I was a step behind him.

"Hope you find him," Tristan called after me. "Hey, let me know if we're still on for tonight!"

The only worker in the Piggly Wiggly was a slight man with a crew cut and a graying mustache working one of the registers. He regarded Austin and me suspiciously as we conferred around the gumball machines. No customers were checking out so I went right up to him while Austin hung back. His nametag read *Store Manager: Bill.*

"Hi, I'm looking for Eli Sutterfield," I said.

"Yeah, you an' me both." He had a toothpick in his mouth that went up and down while he talked. I recognized his voice from the day I'd been hiding in the stockroom.

"So I guess you haven't seen him then?"

His voice got louder. "No, but I can't wait to, so I can far his sorry butt."

Far?"

"Yeah, far. Kick him to the curb. The pink slip." Oh, he meant fire him. The man's face was turning red. "He missed his shift yesterday and there ain't no answer when I call his number."

"Well, his dad's pretty sick."

"Ain't my problem. You his girlfriend?"

"Definitely not." I looked back at Austin, who was inspecting a blinking game with a robot arm to pick up prizes.

"Well, you see him, you tell that boy to get in here so I can far him to his face."

"Okay, I'll let him know." Bill just glared while Austin and I exited the store. We loitered aimlessly for a few minutes on the sun-bleached sidewalk next to the grocery cart corral. "So, where to now?" Austin asked.

"Umm," I said, like the smart person I felt like. We'd washed out. So much for being fated to find Eli. He could be anywhere. Wandering in the woods. Passed out in a ditch somewhere from blood loss. I had no idea where to go next. Still, on the faint hope that Tristan had known what he was talking about, I said, "Let's take a walk behind the store."

"Whatever you want," Austin replied flatly. We trotted around back. Two people sat under the scraggly tree by the chain link fence, one in a wheelchair, one on the ground. Maybe our search was over.

CHAPTER TWENTY-ONE

My frustration was acid in my stomach when we got closer and I saw the figure on the ground wasn't Eli at all, but a girl. Shea sat in her wheelchair, wearing her Piggly Wiggly uniform. Another girl in a pink skirt and blouse and matching high-heeled shoes sat cross-legged at her feet, hunched over like a wilted azalea in the patchy grass.

This other girl raised her head when we drew near. Her eyes were bloodshot and her face flushed, with streaks of make-up running red and blue down her cheeks. She clutched a pink purse in front of her like somebody might grab it and run. It took me several seconds to identify her as Corey's girlfriend, Emily.

"Good morning," Shea called out in a sing-song voice.

"Hi, how are you two?" I asked.

"Ooh, we're fine," Shea said. Emily only sniffled and put her head back down.

"Are you sure?" I asked.

"Well, we have a little situation," Shea said.

Emily let out a ragged, broken breath, as if she'd recently been sobbing. She put a hand on Shea's knee. "It's all right, you can tell them."

Shea patted Emily's hand. "A situation by the name of Corey," she explained. "Emily caught him with another girl this morning." Emily broke down into a fit of sobbing and leaned her head against Shea's leg. Shea stroked Emily's hair and looked up, shaking her head helplessly. "She's been like this for the last half hour."

"God, I'm so sorry, Emily," I said. "What happened?"

Shea spoke for her stricken friend, who moaned and let out big choking gasps of air. "Corey was supposed to pick her up for brunch in Batestown."

"At Ch-Charlene's," Emily got out between sobs.

"Charlene's?" I said.

"Charlene's is where you go if you want to eat fancy," Shea said. "Anyway, Corey never came so Emily went over to his house. It looked like everybody was gone, so Goldilocks here went right in."

"I thought maybe he'd l-left me a note or something," Emily said.

"She heard a noise up in Corey's room, and when shegot up there...." She trailed off.

Now Emily looked up, and her face was contorted and red. "And he was s-supposed to meet my family at brunch! My grandparents! They came down to the festival just to see him!" She broke down again. Shea's pantleg was wet and stained with make-up where she'd been supporting Emily's head.

"Oh my God, that's horrible," I said, hoping I sounded more sympathetic than I felt. A bee buzzed my ear and I brushed it away. The truth was I was a little annoyed. I'd been kidnapped, my brother and I had almost died, my aunt was on her way to jail, and now I was searching for the party responsible for all this because he might be suicidal. Emily's boyfriend problems seemed a little trivial at this point. Controlling my tone of voice, I said, "So, is there anything Austin and I can do?"

"No, but thank you for asking," Emily said in a little voice. "You are too nice." She balled her hands up into fists and pounded them against her knees. "Not like that son-of-a-bitch I've been dating for three years. Oh God, I hate him!"

Austin, standing up until now with his hands in his pockets and tapping a foot impatiently, cleared his throat. "So either of y'all seen Eli?" he asked.

"Eli?" Emily said. "Yeah. The bastard was sitting on the couch at Corey's house. His face was all messed up, too." Her expression contorted. "He knew all along my boyfriend was a two-timing son-of-a-bitch, and he never told me."

My personal guess was that pretty much everybody but Emily knew Corey was a two-timing son-of-a-bitch. I mean, I knew it and I'd only been here two months. But I kept that information to myself. "So you think he's still there?" I asked Emily. I swatted at a bee flying in front of my face.

"No, I waited outside until they left," Emily said. Her tone turned fiercer. "Gone to another state, if he knows what's good for him."

"So we're right back where we started from," Austin muttered to me.

I nodded. That same persistent bee was back, now joined by a second bee, and a minute later a third and a fourth. They weren't trying to sting me, or even land, just circling around my head like they were in orbit or something.

"You must smell sweet," Shea said. "Those honeybees sure love you."

"Geez, they won't leave me alone," I said. Sort of like the honeybees in that dream I'd had about Granddad. What was it Granddad had told me?

Something about listening to the bees to find someone I was looking for.

"Everything all right?" Austin asked.

"Yeah, I'm…listening to the bees."

"Okaay," Shea said. I held a finger to my lips to shush her.

How do you go about listening to a bee? I concentrated on the buzzing. Nothing special in the sound so far as I could tell. I could sense the others glancing at each other but I ignored them and focused on my task.

As I scrutinized the bees, I noticed their movements. They flitted up and down, left and right, at first seemingly at random. But the longer I observed, the more I was able to discern a pattern, a kind of significance, in their movements, and something shifted in my head and I understood them. They were giving me directions. I watched their dance until I had a clear idea in my head of the route we had to take.

"Let's go get in the truck," I said to Austin. "I know where to find them. Eli and Corey both."

"How could you possible know that?" said Shea. "All you've been doing is standing there looking dopey with bugs flying around your head."

"You wouldn't believe me if I told you," I said. Reflexively I touched the bear claw, and was not surprised to find it quite warm.

"Wait, let us come with you," Emily said. "I need to give that jackass a piece of my mind."

"Sorry, babe, I have to stay here and work," Shea said.

"No, Shea! You have to come with me, so I don't talk myself out of it!"

It took Shea all of three seconds to reconsider. "Well, I guess if I'm on Bill's shit list anyway, I might as well go."

The four of us squeezed into the cab of Austin's truck, throwing Shea's wheelchair in the back. There wasn't much talk other than my directions to Austin, only the occasional sniffle or body-wracking sob from Emily. I led us back out of town, down a side road I'd never seen before, and then another. The bees were dead-on accurate so far. We took a hairpin turn around a sheer drop-off. Going over that side would mean a real fast trip to the valley floor, hundreds of feet below.

"Look, over there," I said to Austin, pointing to a red pickup truck parked on the inside shoulder, hugging the rock face of the mountain. Austin guided his truck in behind it. A Dodge Dakota Sport. Yep, it was definitely Eli's.

Didn't seem to be anybody around. I got out and checked. Nobody in the truck. I heard laughing above me and looked up, and there was Corey, about ten feet up, his long legs dangling down from a sort of seat in the side of the rock.

"Hey, it's Eli's freaky girlfriend!" Corey called down. "How'd you find us?"

"You asshole!" screamed Emily, who had climbed out behind me. "I should come up there and push you off that rock!"

"Baby, that girl didn't mean a thing," Corey said.

Emily's face was red with seething. "You think I can't tell you're lying? You never gave a damn about me!"

"Now that's not true at all." He backed his way down the rock face and jumped the last couple feet to the ground. When he spoke again his tones were soft and conciliatory. "I've been thinking about you up there. I never stop thinking about you."

"Then how could you be with another girl?" Emily asked, her voice breaking at the word girl. Tears came to her eyes.

Corey held his arms open. "It's you I care about. You know that. Forget that other slut. I practically had to fight her off me. It's you I want."

Shea called from where she sat in the cab. "Look, you two-timing scum, I hate to interrupt this charming little act of yours, but Austin and Dani are looking for Eli."

Corey glanced at us with surprise, as if he'd forgotten we were here. "Eli? He's up in his aerie."

"His aerie?" Shea said. "What the hell is that? Could you talk like a normal human being for once?"

"I see him," I said, craning my neck. A figure was standing on a ledge way high up, looking straight down at us.

"Now how we gon' get up there?" Austin said. "He's a hundred feet up."

"Don't worry," I said. I almost followed up by saying the bees had explained it all to me, but I stopped myself. There was no need to make Austin doubt my sanity. Instead I simply started climbing. Austin came up behind me.

"Well, I'm sure not going to join you," Shea called to us. "I'll keep an eye on these moron lovebirds."

"Holler if you need anything," Austin yelled back.

The climb was surprisingly easy at first, like scaling a ladder hidden in the rock. The only problem was my injured knee, which protested the pressures and twists. It throbbed and twinged and at one point gave out as I removed one hand from its gripping place, leaving me half dangling in the air. I swiped at the rock with my free hand and was lucky enough to find a grip. It all happened so fast that only when I'd regained my footing did a rush of vertigo pass through me, pushing my heart rate up like I'd run a sprint and leaving my hands clammy and slick.

"What's wrong?" Austin said from below.

"I'm not sure I can go on," I said.

"Keep 'er steady," he said. Something firm in his voice brought me back. I pushed everything down inside myself and proceeded.

At the top a broad ledge was formed where the rock face jogged back a few yards. When I came over the side, Eli was standing on the far edge, his boots off and his toes curled right over the ledge's lip. His face was crimson, as if he'd been crying.

I took a few steps towards him. "Stop right there," Eli cried out. From behind, Austin grabbed my arm.

I stopped. Damn it. I was so angry and now I'd finally found him. I wanted nothing more than to curse Eli out for about an hour, beat on his chest, knock him down and kick him over and over. And now he had to pull this crap. Still, we couldn't have him jumping, I guess.

I forced myself to speak evenly and soothingly. "Stay calm, Eli. Don't do anything to hurt yourself." There'd be time to yell at him after we'd talked him back.

"Ain't me I'm worried about," he said.

"Take a look at your feet," Austin whispered to

me, his hand still gripping my arm.

I looked down. In a little crevice right next to where I'd been about to step, a huge striped snake lay curled up in a patch of sun, its flat, triangular head resting on top of its coils, its slitted eyes regarding me without blinking. Its tail stuck out from underneath: a rattle.

"A timber rattler," Eli called out. "Beauty, ain't she?"

CHAPTER TWENTY-TWO

Down in the valley, an ocean of green stretched as far as the eye could see, the waves of forest breaking here and there into little foamy white and brown flecks of human activity. Smoke rose from the chimney of a little cabin. A couple cars crept along a ribbon of highway. Kids ran on a baseball field, hazy in the distance. Down there, life went on as normal. Up here, life seemed very precarious indeed. The snake flicked out its tongue, its mouth only inches from my leg. I was wearing jeans but had the distinct feeling the snake knew enough to strike someplace my skin was exposed.

I tried to speak but my mouth was dry. After a couple attempts, I managed to croak out a response. "Beautiful's not the word I had in mind."

"Don't move a muscle," Eli called back. As if I

could.

"I reckon you're pissed about what I did to you an' your brother."

"You reckon right."

"Well, I knew you two'd get out all right."

"I'm so glad to hear you have that much faith in us." I had to physically unclench my teeth to say it.

Eli stepped back from the edge and squatted. "This part's a little tricky," he said. "No sudden moves." He slapped the ground twice with one hand. The snake unhurriedly advanced out of its tanning bed, its long body lazily uncoiling. I drew in my breath as it glided smoothly by my shoes. It was fully as long as a grown man, its body so big around I couldn't have held it in my hands with my fingers touching. It brushed its head against Eli's leg and curled around his bare feet. Eli looked up and spoke. "You see you ain't the only one with a buddy from the wild kingdom." He chuckled. "You two can step closer now."

I didn't move and neither did Austin, except for him releasing his grip on my arm. "You know people were looking for us?" I said. "The sheriff and everything?" It was disconcerting speaking to him with the serpent writhing around his body, one moment at his feet, the next up around his thighs and waist, its body undulating and its little tongue flicking in and out all the time.

"Was they now? Huh. I was missin' too and wasn't nobody lookin' for me."

"Get off your high horse, Sutterfield," Austin growled from behind me. "We was lookin' for you same as Dani an' Ryan. Nobody knew it was you who kidnapped 'em. And even after they showed up, we still been lookin' for you all mornin'."

"Huh," Eli said. His chin dropped a little lower, as if he'd been deflated of a little of his self-righteousness. I took a couple tentative steps. "Don't worry," he said, softer. "This big girl ain't gon' hurt you." He ran his hand along the rattler's scaled body. The snake did seem to respond, almost with…affection?

Very, very cautiously I advanced to Eli. Blood from where Ryan had stabbed him with the arrowhead encrusted the thigh of his jeans. The cuts on his right cheek were spotted with yellowish pus. His clothes were dirty, his hair matted, his eyes rimmed with red.

"Jesus, you're a mess," I said. I pulled a tissue out from my pocket and held it out to him. The snake's head darted in my direction, but Eli put a hand on its body and the head drew back.

He took the tissue and dabbed at his cheek. "Now you see, Dani. How I knew you been talkin' with bears. How I knew you'd get out of that cave. 'Cause

I knew you was like me."

I glanced back at Austin. He remained several steps back, watching the whole scene with a wary eye. I turned back to Eli. "Am I like you?" I asked. Not sarcastically; my question was genuine. Obviously he had a connection with an animal, like Aunt Eunice and me. But a heron was one thing, or a bear. What kind of connection could a person have with a snake?

"You know, I first met this lady after the accident." Eli stroked the rattler again. I had to admit its coloring was gorgeous: orangish-black bands patterned over a dusky yellow, more vibrant than any painting or Persian rug. "You don't know what happened to my mama, do you?"

I shook my head.

"She was hit by a car. Five years ago."

"I'm sorry," I said.

"Mama survived the original accident. Went home that night. Mild concussion, they said. A few scratches and scrapes. The next day, she goes into Doc Moser's office complainin' of a headache, and come out on a stretcher. She died before the ambulance reached Batestown." The snake actually put its head on Eli's shoulder and fixed me with its cold gaze. "You know, all this time I been blamin' him. Your granddaddy, I mean."

"I never knew," I said, staring right back into those

emotionless eyes. The forked tongue flicked out and in. "I'm sure my grandfather did everything he could."

"Not just your grandfather. Anybody who got in my way, I been blamin'. Preacher Joab. He bein' a man of God and all, so why didn't he do nothin' to stop it?" I heard Austin shift behind me. "Hell, I been blamin' God hisself for what happened. 'Specially now that He put Daddy in the same situation."

I didn't say anything.

Eli turned his head and inhaled deeply, as if to compose himself. "It all made so much sense, Dani. You bein' Doc Moser's granddaughter. The bear claw. Your brother. It all seemed so perfect." His voice grew kind of distant. "And I would've done anythin' I could to help Daddy."

"You know, Enos probably wants to see you," Austin said. "A visit from you'd probably mean more to him than anything right now."

"Daddy died at 6:12 this morning," Eli said flatly.

That stopped the conversation cold for a good long while. Eli sat and slipped on his boots while Austin and I stood, stunned.

"Oh, God," I murmured finally. 6:12 was about when Ryan and I had emerged from the cave. Enos must have expired at the time Ryan and I had broken the surface of the water. Maybe the exact moment.

"I'm so sorry," Austin said. His words were quiet but clear in the still air.

Time to change the subject. "You know, we really should get you some attention for your leg and face," I said to Eli. "Medical attention. It looks like it's getting infected."

Eli shook his head. He put his hand around the snake's head and lifted it. The tongue flicked. "Look at her eye. See anything strange?"

I shook my head. "I don't know what you're getting at," I said.

"It's milky," Austin called out. And he was right, the snake's eyes did have a sort of white film over them.

"Means she's fixin' to molt," Eli said, rising to his feet. "Lose her old skin. Come out all new and shiny. You ever wish you could do the same thing?"

"Of course," I said. "All the time, actually."

"Yeah?" Eli said. "Me too." He lifted his boot and smashed it hard on the snake's skull. The crunch echoed off the rocks. The long body writhed a minute under Eli's heel, wrapping around his legs, and stopping with a shudder. I stared with my mouth agape.

Eli's eyes were fierce. "Long enough," he said. "This lady been whisperin' in my ear long enough, tellin' me who all to blame. But it wasn't your granddaddy's fault. It wasn't Preacher Joab's fault neither. I ain't lettin' God off the hook yet, but maybe I can talk it over with him."

I wanted to say something but had no idea what that might be.

Eli shook the lifeless coils off his feet and stepped out. "Ain't you still mad at me?" he asked.

I shook my head. I truly wasn't, not anymore. I really just felt sorry for him.

"Dani?" he asked. "Yes?"

Eli looked me in the eye, and now, of all the unexpected things that happened that morning, that whole weekend, maybe the whole summer, I think this is the one thing that surprised me most.

"I'm ready to shed my old skin," he said. "I been angry so long. I want to let it go. But Mama's gone. And Daddy's gone. And I ain't got no place to go." And he began to weep. I took him in my arms and he leaned against me and sobbed like a little boy.

CHAPTER TWENTY-THREE

I know Austin felt pretty awkward, standing there, keeping his eyes anywhere but on Eli and me. He kicked at a pebble which tumbled down the rock face and hopped across the road far below while Eli pressed his face into my shoulder. When he recovered himself we descended.

The climb down was easier than it had been going up, though by the time we got to the bottom my knee was killing me. We found Corey and Emily sitting in the grass, Corey with his arm around her back and she nuzzling her head into his shoulder while he murmured to her. They barely seemed to notice our arrival. Shea leaned her head against the window frame of Eli's truck with a cigarette between two fingers and a disgusted look on her face.

"I tried to talk her out of it," she said to us. "But he started sweet-talkin' her and ten minutes later they're sittin' together like nothin' ever happened."

"It's the same every time," Austin said. "Some people can't never change."

"But some people can," I added, under my breath.

"I don't know how long he'll get away with it before she catches on," Shea said. She tossed the cigarette away. "So, Austin, can you give me a ride to the Pig? I might have a chance to keep my job if I get back soon."

"I'll take you," Eli said.

"You sure?" Austin asked. "You okay with drivin'?"

"Yeah, I'm good," he said. He nodded at Austin. I took the friendly gesture to be a good sign. "I'll pick up iodine or somethin' for my face and leg. I can drop the lovebirds off on the way too." He climbed in the driver's seat of his truck, his face grimacing when he swung his hurt leg up. He rolled down the window and called to me. "Hey, we still on for tonight? Seven o'clock, right?"

It took me a moment even to realize what he was talking about. The concert. "Are you kidding?" I asked. "You're still going to try to play? With your wounds? And your...you know?"

"Daddy would've wanted me to play," he said. "I'll be there."

So it was just Austin and me on the way back. The ride was quiet but not tense. It was…peaceful. Comfortable. Austin was good that way. He turned the corner at the farming equipment store and I gasped when I saw what was waiting in the front yard of the rental house: a white BMW with Minnesota plates.

Mom.

PART FIVE:
PIECE OF MY HEART

CHAPTER TWENTY-FOUR

I barely waited for Austin's truck to roll to a stop before jumping out.

"Thanks for the ride, see you later," I called back over my shoulder, and I was out and up the steps to the house before I think Austin even knew what was happening. Not too dignified but I didn't care at that moment. Austin would have to understand.

Mom was sitting on the couch leafing through a magazine and rose as soon as she saw me. "Oh, Dani, I'm so glad you're safe," she said, gathering me in her arms.

"Mom, I can't believe you came down!"

"Of course I came down!" she said. "I was on my way last night as soon as your father told me you and Ryan were missing."

I let her hold me and it was kind of like I was a little girl again, for a minute, pressed against her and breathing in her mom smell. I don't know how other mothers smell but mine is a combination of perfume, designer clothes, sugar-free gum, Chinese take-out, late nights at the office, and barely-made deadlines. It's not always a perfect smell but it was just what I needed right then.

From the hallway Dad appeared. He stood off to the side, a little awkward. "So did you find him?" he asked when Mom and I parted.

"Yeah, we found him," I said.

"How's he doing?"

"His father died this morning. His face is torn up and he has a stab wound in his leg that might be infected. Plus I think he's lost his job at the Pig. But he's surprisingly upbeat about it."

"Who's this?" Mom asked. "Are you talking about the boy that kidnapped you and Ryan?"

"Yeah, Eli," I said. "He's changed though. He was confused because his father was sick, and…" I trailed off. How could I possibly explain it? Before I could start, something else popped in my head. "Oh, and you have to come see me play at seven, I'm doing a song for the folk festival with Eli and this other guy, Tristan." But that wasn't even the most important thing. "And, oh my God, Aunt Eunice is in trouble.

The sheriff's deputies were at her house because she was growing pot. They arrested her and we have to help her and we can't forget Ruskin because—"

"Slow down, Dani," Mom said. "Take a deep breath and explain it all slowly."

And then I simply laughed, because I had so much on my mind and my brain was whirring and no matter what I tried to say it all came out in one big jumble. I was starting to sound like Ryan. I collapsed on the couch laughing so hard that Mom and Dad looked at me like I was crazy. Maybe I was.

Mom questioned whether I should be playing that evening after all the events of the previous twenty-four hours and no sleep, but I insisted I'd been rehearsing for weeks and wasn't tired at all. Actually, I was starting to feel the lack of sleep a little bit, but I knew if I slowed down now, even to close my eyes for a second, I might not get up again for hours, or maybe days. And there was still the matter of Aunt Eunice, so Mom and I drove in the BMW to Batestown to bail her out. Odd. Who could have predicted it would be me going to get her out of jail and not the other way around?

The wait at the county lockup was tedious. Mom

had to fill out reams of paperwork about paying bail while I sat on the most uncomfortable wooden bench ever built. An overworked air conditioner failed to keep the temperature under eighty and the room stank of body odor and Lysol. Depressed people sat around anxious and sullen, mostly mothers and girlfriends it looked like, with their unwashed hair and day-old clothes and screaming toddlers. The wait was only forty-five minutes but felt like hours and hours.

Finally, Mom finished up and the guard brought Aunt Eunice out. She looked almost... humbled. Stooped shoulders and a tired face. She glanced around the room, spotted us waiting for her, and straightened the feather in her hair.

"It's a pleasure to see you, Deborah," she said with a tired smile. "And I thank y'all for coming to get me."

"Nonsense. Are you hungry?" Mom asked, pushing open the heavy security door into the corridor.

"I am starved. I missed lunch and they had nothing for us in the holding cell," she said as we strode past the metal detector. The heavy front door of the jail closed behind us.

On the broad courthouse lawn, Aunt Eunice wavered a moment and then embraced Mom and me. Her face was brighter and she was back to her regular self. "I am truly sorry to have caused you such a fuss, Deborah," she said, still holding us. "I never thought we would meet again like this."

"I'm happy to do it," Mom said. "Where can we eat around here?"

"We could go to Charlene's," I said. Mom and Aunt Eunice looked at me. "I hear it's where you go when you want to eat fancy."

Charlene's turned out to be a little café in a restored old Victorian house with the soup and sandwich of the day listed on a chalkboard. It was only a couple doors down from the hotel I'd become so well acquainted with two nights before, although now that seemed like months ago. A waitress in a crisp white uniform seated us on a shady veranda surrounded by rose bushes. Ice tinkled in glasses of sweet tea and silverware clinked against china.

"Are you all right after your ordeal?" Mom asked, spreading her napkin in her lap.

"Why certainly," Aunt Eunice said. "I met the most interesting young lady in the holding cell. Tattoos all up and down her arms. She said she was in for writing bad checks. Not too much older than Dani. Can you believe that?"

"Mmm-hmm," Mom said, stirring her iced tea.

"Twenty-two and she'd done time twice already, she told me. And to think, here I am, sixty-one years old and this is the first time I've been in trouble with the law in my life. Never even a speeding ticket."

"That's exactly what I'm counting on, Eunice," Mom said. "So, is it true what Dani tells me? That you were growing marijuana on your land?" I knew the tone of voice—easy, almost friendly, but with a hint that the answer had better not be wrong. I think she's perfected it over years of working with clients.

"Well, yes, it's true," Aunt Eunice said. "Last night, when they were searching for the kids, it seems one of the deputies came across it."

"I see," Mom said. "But doesn't marijuana grow wild in these parts?"

"Oh, I told them it was mine," Aunt Eunice said. Mom groaned. "I know you think that was foolish, but I'm too old to start lying now, and anyway the deputy was so friendly I didn't think a thing of it. My mind was on Dani and Ryan, you understand. But this morning they came back. They had a search warrant with them. Now they've rummaged through my house like it's a junk store and I believe they even ransacked my garden, though I didn't have a chance to check."

The waitress interrupted us to bring our food.

Chef's salad for Mom. Vegetable soup and sun-dried tomato platter for Aunt Eunice. Egg salad on rye for me. The conversation resumed when she left.

"Oh, Eunice, it's a good thing I'm here," Mom said. "How much marijuana were you growing back there?"

"Six plants. I don't need that much for myself. But I grow it for the local medical marijuana club, you see."

And then it dawned on me. The bags of vegetables Eli picked up every week. Apparently they contained more than just peppers and cucumbers, but also the cure his father needed for his lack of appetite. And undoubtedly the source of Eli's own stash, as well. I wondered if Aunt Eunice knew about that little diversion of her supply.

"But medical marijuana's not legal in Arkansas," Mom said. Aunt Eunice's face took on a pained expression. "I see. I suppose you told them what you do with it?"

"No, it never came up," Aunt Eunice said.

"Well, that's one good thing, at least," Mom said. "From now on we answer no more questions until we're in front of a judge. And certainly not without me or another lawyer there with you. Understand?"

"Yes, I do," Aunt Eunice said. "How much trouble am I in, Deborah?"

"Oh, Eunice," Mom said. "It depends on so many things—"

Aunt Eunice looked Mom in the eye and tapped the table with her index finger. "Do not mince words or offer me false hope, Deborah. I want the real truth."

"Fair enough," Mom said. She hesitated a moment, then plunged in. "I'm not familiar with the law in Arkansas, but that amount will be considered proof of intent to distribute. In the worst case, you could be looking at five to ten years."

"Oh, my." Aunt Eunice slumped in her chair. Her face had flushed, and she held her hand to her chest. Mom pushed her chair back and stood, but Aunt Eunice motioned her back down. "I'm fine, dear. But I must say, the news is a little shocking."

"Now, Eunice," Mom said. "There are all sorts of reasons it might not be that much. We're working with a spotless record. And you're an older lady, respected in the community. With luck, any jail time should be suspended or you could serve it at home. If you think you can keep out of trouble for a few years."

"Well, I can't imagine what kind of trouble it would be. But then, I never thought this would happen either." Aunt Eunice reached over and put one hand on Mom's hand. "Thank you for not holding back, Deborah. I appreciate that." She drew back and took a sip of tea. "Well, now. Five to ten years. It certainly would put a crimp in one's gardening plans, wouldn't it?"

Mom laughed. "I imagine it would."

"But enough talk," Aunt Eunice said. "We need to hurry up and eat so we can get our girl back in time for her show." She swallowed a sun-dried tomato and held her fork up at an angle to punctuate her next words. "You are in for a treat tonight, Deborah. Your daughter has been practicing with the boys for weeks. It's a good thing y'all bailed me out, because otherwise there would have been a jailbreak. I will tell you, nothing is going to keep me from seeing Dani play tonight."

CHAPTER TWENTY-FIVE

I slouched with Eli and Tristan on a stone table outside an antique store. We were due on in forty-five minutes. The two boys wore their embroidered shirts and clean blue jeans, Eli with his usual Razorbacks cap and three parallel wounds across his cheek, cleaned up but still raw-looking. Tristan wore a gray cowboy hat, an old- fashioned touch that still somehow matched his tats and long hair. I had on a simple white blouse and blue jeans and Aunt Eunice had done my hair in a half updo with a couple stalks of Queen Anne's lace, which also served to artfully hide the bare spot.

I'd fought a bout of sleepiness on the way back from Batesville but now, as performance time got closer, a queasy, nervous energy grew in me. "You two get butterflies in your stomach before going on stage?" I asked my partners while we watched all the folks pass by. A lot of people would be in the audience.

Tristan laughed. "Definitely. Happens to everybody."

"Are you sure? 'Cause I think I might puke."

"That bad, huh?" Tristan opened his dulcimer case and pulled out a brown paper bag. He passed it to me. Inside was a jam jar filled with a clear liquid. It didn't look like medicine. "Take a couple sips of that, little bird," he instructed.

I screwed off the top and sniffed it. Definitely alcohol but didn't smell of much else. "What is it? Vodka or something?"

"Better than that," Tristan said. "But sip it slowly." Out of the corner of my eye I saw him and Eli grinning. I was glad to see Eli in a good mood as he'd been withdrawn and mute since we'd gotten here. Understandably so.

I took a little test sip and felt it roll across my tongue and down my throat, wet but more viscous than water and somehow scalding hot and cool at the same time. A smell kind of like turpentine rose up through my nose. I shook my head involuntarily. "What the hell?"

"Congratulations, babe. You just had your first

taste o' genuine Arkansas moonshine," Eli said. It was the first words he'd spoken since we'd parted earlier. If this is what it took to cheer him up, it might be worth it.

"This can't be healthy," I said. I took another sip. It went down a little easier, if only because my tongue was numb from the first time. "Good news. The butterflies are gone. I think I killed them. Where'd you get this stuff?"

"It's easy, if you know who to ask," Tristan said. "Buddy of mine brings a batch down to the festival every year. Makes a killing on it."

I passed the jar to Eli, who took a sip and handed it to Tristan. We traded it back and forth and after fifteen minutes the jar was half gone.

I sat there feeling good at first but soon nausea spread from the steaming pool in my stomach throughout my body. I knew I was going to be sick real soon. I struggled to my feet and pushed my way into the crowd, unsteadily shouldering my way through to the Cultural Center.

There was a line about a block long outside the women's restroom but none outside the men's. Typical. I hesitated a moment but there was no help for it so I kicked open the door to the men's room and hit the stall just in time to spray a cascade of Ozark firewater and bile. "Oh, shit," I murmured, pressing my hands against the sides of the stall to keep from falling over.

"Dani, is that you?" came a hoarse voice from the next stall. "Yeah, it's me. Who the hell are you?"

The door of my stall opened and I whirled around. There stood Austin, dressed all in black like Johnny Cash. I immediately regretted the whirling because it stirred up my stomach again and I turned right back for another round.

"Yeah, that's what I was up to," Austin said, handing me a tissue from his pocket after I finished painting the commode again.

"Oh, it didn't sound like you," I said. "You drink some of that poison they're calling moonshine too?"

Austin laughed. "Nah. I always get an upset stomach before I perform."

"You're performing?"

"Yep, fiddle. I'm on in ten minutes." He looked a little shy, kind of half-smiled. "You gon' watch me?"

"Yeah, sure. Of course. If you watch me too." I felt a little guilty. How many times had I looked over the schedule and never noticed Austin's name on there? He must have been only two or three slots ahead of me. A little self-absorbed, are we?

A bearded guy with a big beer belly walked in the restroom and gave me an odd glance before sidling up to a urinal. He let out a belch and unzipped his pants.

"Well, I'd better go get ready," Austin said. I followed him out and through the crowd. At the edge of the stage a man with a clipboard leaned over and whispered something to Austin, who whispered back. I found a free chair near the front and settled in to watch.

When it was Austin's turn he mounted the stage. He glanced nervously around the room, his eyes squinted against the glare of the stage lights. I wondered if he was looking for me until I saw Joab sitting not far away, clapping with his beefy hands. He caught Austin's eye and gave him a wave. The emcee came to the microphone. "And our next act is Austin Campbell, playing 'Fog on the Mountain' on his fiddle." More applause than I expected, a couple hoots from the crowd. It'd gotten a lot more crowded in the room in the last few minutes.

Austin put his bow to a string and I winced at the cat- yowling screech it produced. He stopped, his face a mask of calm, reapplied the bow, and started playing for real. And I do mean for real. The song was a true bluegrass breakdown and he took it at a breakneck tempo, but still hitting each note clean, reeling off double stops and triplets, his eyes closed while his fingers played across the fretboard like heat-seeking missiles locked on their targets. Three minutes and it was over, not a single flubbed note.

There was a surge of applause and whooping that sounded like a thunderstorm opening up. Austin took a handkerchief from his pocket to wipe his forehead. He put his mouth up to the microphone. "Thanks y'all for listening." Joab met him as he stepped down from the stage, embracing him in a bear hug that nearly knocked Austin to the floor. Even above the clapping I could hear his booming voice. "You done good boy, you done good!"

A tap on my shoulder. Tristan, looking relieved. "There you are. We thought you'd be back by now. We're on in ten."

"Oh, sorry about that." "You feeling better?"

"Yeah, I just stopped to see Austin play."

"He's damn good, huh?"

"Yeah, he is. I didn't even know he played fiddle until earlier today."

Tristan raised his eyebrows. "Seriously? You didn't know he played? Shit, Dani. He went up to the National Fiddle Contest in Weiser, Idaho, last year. Came in second in the junior division."

"Huh." I looked over. Austin had broken free of his dad and was talking to a group of younger kids. One kid handed him a notepad and a pen. Austin took it and wrote something. Was he signing autographs? I shook my head, trying to process the fact that Austin was famous, at least around here. He'd previously seemed so shy. Unassuming. A little dull, even. Could it be he was actually just humble?

No time to consider the matter longer. Mom, Dad, and Aunt Eunice appeared from somewhere in the crowd. Even Ryan was with them, rubbing sleep from his eyes. Mom gave me a kiss on the cheek. "Almost time. You ready?"

"As ready as I can be, I guess."

"You'll do great, Danielle," she said, brushing a stray strand of hair from my face.

Eli stepped up and touched my arm. It was time. Dad put a hand on my shoulder. "Well, break a leg." He paused, then said, "You too, Eli."

"Thank you, Mr. Moser," Eli said. He turned to me and said, "Come on, let's tune up."

Tristan, Eli, and I took the stage right on time. The stage lights were super bright. All eyes in the crowd were raised to the stage expectantly. This was it. No fantasy of Janis at Monterey. This was the real thing. Dani Moser at Adelaide. The emcee at the microphone spoke: "And now, the Gin Soaked Boys, with special guest Dani Moser, playing their version of *Hangman Slack Your Rope*."

Eli started in with the chords on his guitar and I began to sing. As soon as the song was underway I forgot all about the nervousness. The stage lights

actually helped in that regard because I could hardly
see beyond the first row of tables. Only the music
existed, the intoxication of our voices melding and
our instruments intertwining. We'd worked it up
with Eli and me trading off little descending riffs in
between the verses while Tristan arpeggiated on the
dulcimer over us. I took the first part of each verse:

> *Hangman, slack your rope a while*
> *I think I see my brother,*
> *Comin' a-many mile.*
> *Brother, did you bring a silver cup?*
> *Did you bring a purse full of gold?*
> *Or did you come to see me,*
> *swingin' from the gallows pole?*

And so I sang, appealing to my brother, my uncle,
and my father as the verses progressed. And Tristan
or Eli answered each time:

> *Sister, I have no silver cup,*
> *I brought no purse full of gold*
> *I just came to see you,*
> *swingin' from the gallows pole.*

And then the final verse, when I appealed to Eli for
help:

> *Lover, have you brought a white veil,*
> *and a ring of gold?*
> *Have you come to pledge your love,*
> *and save me from the gallows pole?*

And Eli replied:

> *Lover, I brought a white veil,*
> *and a ring of gold.*
> *I came to take your hand,*
> *and save you from the gallows pole.*

He gave me a grin and I flashed one back. We'd pulled it off. We closed out the song with the final guitar licks. The room was silent for a beat, and then the clapping started, spreading until the whole place was applauding. I stepped down from the stage, squinting in the full glare of the stage lights and then standing in a daze while my eyes adjusted to the relative dark beyond. I felt somebody hugging me, heard Dad saying, "Dani, that was just great. I am so proud of you." And I smiled, because he hadn't had too many occasions in the past year to say he was proud of me.

CHAPTER TWENTY-SIX

The only reason I stayed awake through dinner was because I wanted to be with Mom. After thirty-six straight hours without sleep I can't say I was much of a conversationalist. I'm surprised I didn't wind up face down in my food. As soon as the dishes were cleared I was back in the old Arctic chill room, curled up under the quilt as protection against the extreme air conditioning, and out in an instant. I slept hard, the way a marathon runner sleeps after the race, or a soldier after the battle. Or, maybe, a bear after summer is through and it settles down to hibernate in its hidden place.

When I opened my eyes I expected it to be morning, but in fact it was dark out and the world was silent. I felt a familiar feeling compelling me out of bed. I couldn't have resisted it if I'd tried, but I didn't try. I rose and glided silently through the house. Dad was asleep on the couch in the living room. Too bad he wasn't in the bedroom with Mom, but I guess I wasn't surprised. I crept along, trying each step before putting my weight down so as to avoid creaky floorboards. I carefully unlatched the screen door and made my way down the porch steps and around the back.

The ground under my bare feet alternated between mossy soft and pine straw prickly, and the air was crisper than it had been all summer, a little preview of fall in the mountains. My legs carried me deep into the woods, away from the cluster of houses, far from human habitation.

Unlike my last nighttime excursion this night was moonlit and I saw her silhouette well before reaching the spot where she waited. She stood upright, a full eight or nine feet tall. Luxurious black fur hung on her like a theater curtain. Her massive paws seemed big enough to cause thunder should she bring them together. Her. The bear. *My* bear.

I wasn't nervous like last time yet still I did not dare gaze at her face. As before, when she spoke it was a voice without sound, resonating inside my head. "You are safe now and the ones you love are with you," she said. A simple statement of fact, but the words struck me deep in my core as an affirmation of what was true in the world.

"Yes," I said, startling myself with my own, actual, out- loud voice. It occurred to me I owed her my gratitude. "Thank you for giving me your strength. There was no way I could have done it on my own."

"I did not give you my strength," she said. "I only unlocked what was already inside you. But no matter: your ordeal is over, and you have done well."

"But it's not over," I said. I knew I was pushing my luck, but I had to try. "Not all the way. My Aunt Eunice is in trouble with the law and might go to jail."

"Ah," she said, and was quiet a moment. "I have watched your aunt a long time. She does not deserve such treatment. But that matter is in the realm of man, and I have no power to assist you."

I nodded. I hadn't really expected her to help with that anyway. What would we do, take a bear in the courtroom? Now another request formed in my mind, one I hesitated to put forward because I was not sure if she would like it. I screwed up my courage. "May I touch you?" I asked.

"You may, child," she said.

So I reached out and touched her fur, right on her side. It was somewhat coarse, but warm. I put both my arms around her, and she put her arms around me, enveloping me, a literal bear hug. And I felt her breath again, as before, hot and sweet and aromatic, starting on the top of my head and flowing over me. It was strange in that embrace, knowing she could crush me in a second if she wanted, and yet I had never been in a presence so gentle.

"Are you an angel?" I asked, my face buried in her fur.

In my mind I felt a shaking sort of sensation and I realized she was laughing. "Child, I am no angel," she said. "I serve Him who commands angels, as most beasts do, and some men still as well. And I am also a bear, and you know I am real because you are holding me."

"But if you're a bear, how can you talk to me?"

More laughing. "I am of my kind, and I am also the sum of my kind, and their spirits flow through me. In the right place, some of your kind can share in the spirit flow and find a special ally among the beasts, each according to the nature of his soul. If you cannot understand this, do not let it trouble you." She released me and I stepped back. She turned as if to leave. But she couldn't go yet, I still had too many questions.

"Wait!" I said. "How did my grandfather know I would need you? Where did he get the bear claw?"

She regarded me with what I felt was a touch of impatience. "Your grandfather was a steward of this land and a healer. He learned the ways that are now almost forgotten. Even now he watches over you through the eyes of those creatures with whom he shared a special bond."

"The bees," I said, under my breath. Of course. Louder I said, "So if he's watching me, does that mean Granddad is still alive?"

"He is not alive," she said. "But nor is he gone. And now we have spoken long enough, child, and I must go."

I had more questions, many more, but I knew question time was at an end. "Thank you," I said. "Will I ever see you again?"

"All things are possible. But you have the claw around your neck. That belongs to you forever." And with that, she fell to all fours and ambled off into the trees. I stood without moving for many minutes. The cicada drone rose and fell around me, and in the distance an owl hooted. I felt myself very alone, but very peaceful. Although I was not nearly as alone as I had thought.

There was a rustling behind me and I spun around, extremely surprised to see Ryan standing behind me, dressed only in a t-shirt and underpants. "Ryan!" I said in a loud whisper, although I don't know who I thought I would disturb. "What are you doing out here?"

"I heard you leave the house," he said. "I saw you go out the front door and I followed you."

"So you were snooping on me?" I said.

"I was afraid," he said, his voice little and quiet. "I thought somebody might try to hurt you, like Eli did in the cave."

"Oh, Ryan," I said, tears coming to my eyes as my irritation melted away. I hugged him and held him close, and he put his thin little arms around me as well.

"Was that a real bear?" he asked, leaning his head on my chest.

"Yes. Yes, it was."

"Are you friends with him?" he asked.

"Yes. And it's a she."

"Can I meet her sometime?"

I laughed. "Maybe. I don't know if I'll ever see her again, myself."

"If you do, I want to be with you," he said.

I let him go. "We'll see," I said. "Who knows, maybe you'll have your own animal someday. C'mon, let's go back. I'll tell you about her on the way." And we started back toward the house, hand in hand.

CHAPTER TWENTY-SEVEN

Mom left at six o'clock sharp the next morning. I think her plan was to drive all day, arrive in Minneapolis around dinner, and head straight to the office to check her email. Crazy lady. Ryan and I got up early to see her off. And maybe I'm reading too much into this, but before she left, she and Dad kissed in the yard. Not a French kiss or anything, but he had his arms around her and the kiss was on the lips, lingering for a few seconds. A good sign, right?

Ryan and I went back in to get some more sleep. When I woke again in late morning, Dad was standing alone on the porch, looking off into the trees. Had he even come in since she'd left? I stood next to him. He put his arm around my shoulder.

"How are things going with your bear?" he asked.

Not the subject I had expected him to bring up. "Um, fine," I said. "I saw her last night, actually."

"Really?"

I nodded but didn't say anything.

"It's okay," he said. "You don't have to tell me what happened. It's private between you two."

A hummingbird flitted around the honeysuckle intertwined with the railing. It buzzed up and down, left and right, sticking its long beak down the trumpet- shaped flowers, not noticing or caring about the two humans right above it.

Dad gave a little smile as he observed the bird. "You know, I had a friend of my own at one time."

"An animal friend?" I asked.

"That's right. I probably never would have met your mother if I hadn't."

This was interesting. "What do you mean?"

"Oh, it's complicated," he said. "It's no big secret I didn't get along too well with your grandfather."

"Yeah. Aunt Eunice told me a little about it."

"She should know," he said. "She was in the middle of it enough. She always had the right words to calm us down. But she couldn't be around for every fight."

"What did you fight about?" I asked.

"Oh, everything. I thought Daddy was too rigid, I guess. Of course it was my fault too. Thought I knew everything. Didn't care what some old man thought about my life. Not that you'd have any idea about that, eh?" He gave me a wink.

"Maybe it runs in the family," I said, grinning self-consciously.

"You aren't a tenth as bad as I was," he continued. "But I had cause to be. The old man used to be on my case all the time. Every moment had to be devoted to something productive. Studying. Chores. Church. Mow the lawn. Clear the brush. Hit the books. Like taking a moment to relax was a sin or something. It wasn't the kind of life I wanted for myself, then or now."

"But what does that have to do with your animal?"

"I'm getting there," he said, holding a finger up. "One morning we had a real knock-down, drag-out fight. Must have yelled myself hoarse trying to get my point through the old man's thick head. Now I don't even remember what the fuss was about. I slammed the front door and went for a walk. Walked all day, deep into the hills. Wasn't sure I was ever going back. But when I stopped, there it was." The hummingbird hovered right in front of us for a moment, as if it'd overheard our conversation, blinked, and went back to its flowers.

"What was it?" I asked.

"Why, a ruby-throated hummingbird, Dani. Just

like this one."

"Your animal was a hummingbird?" I was surprised it would be such a small animal. But then, Dad did have a tendency to flitter, to make sudden gestures and decisions, to buzz all around. Yeah, I could see it.

"Oh, it was absolutely gorgeous. The most brilliant colors you could imagine. And the strangest thing was, he spoke to me. Not out loud, but I could understand him, if that makes any sense."

"I know exactly what you mean," I said.

"Well, I guess you would." Dad put a hand on the wooden railing. "After that first day, whenever I needed companionship, I'd head out for some sunny place where wildflowers grew, and there he'd be, gathering nectar. He listened when no one else would."

"But how did that lead to Mom?"

"Mom, right. So, you know hummingbirds migrate in the winter, right?"

"Sure. They go to Mexico or some place, I think."

"Exactly," he said. "Well, my hummingbird suggested I do the same thing."

"Go to Mexico?"

Dad gave me a look. "Don't be so literal, Danielle. I mean, hummingbirds travel every year so they can live someplace they feel more comfortable. And I felt trapped here, in tiny little Adelaide, with no prospects. I was miserable. So he gave me the idea to do the same thing."

"Find someplace more to your liking?"

"Exactly. Best advice I ever got. I got out a map and picked a place. Minneapolis. Knew nothing about it, except it was far away from here. Sounded exotic. I met your mother the very week I arrived there, and the rest is history."

"Without him, Ryan and I might even not be here now," I said.

"Good point," Dad said. "I hadn't thought of that. You know, I hoped maybe I would see my little guy this summer."

The hummingbird took off and darted behind the house without so much as glance back. "Maybe this one will tell your friend you're visiting."

"Maybe," he said. "But I doubt it. It kind of seems like these guys show up at times in your life when you need a little extra help."

"Well, Dad," I said, hesitantly. "Things have been tough for you lately."

Dad laughed. "You're right. Not the best year of my life. Mom. The job. The house. You know what's worried me most lately, though?"

I shook my head.

"You, Danielle," he said. "But you know what? I think you've done a lot of maturing this summer. So maybe I don't need that hummingbird, anyhow."

"Thanks, Dad," I said. I gave him a hug and went in for breakfast.

So Dad thought I'd grown up a little. I mulled that over the rest of the week. Maybe he was right. Yes, I'd done some dumb things and gotten in trouble. And gotten Ryan and Aunt Eunice mixed up in it as well. But I knew I was different now than at the beginning of the summer. Turns out spending the night in some dark, forlorn, God-forsaken place, not knowing if you'll live through the end of it, has a way of giving you perspective. Little brothers and bad hair mishaps don't seem so important anymore. It does really degrade your opinion of the hot guy who put you in that situation, though.

Speaking of Eli, I'd probably better explain what happened to him, which leads us back to Austin and Joab. The night before I headed back home, Eunice and I stopped by the Campbells' to deliver a Tupperware full of elderberry flower fritters. I'd never been to Austin's house. It was down the end of a dirt road, a ramshackle place with a goat nibbling on weeds out front. I heard chickens in the backyard. Even more rustic than I'd expected.

Austin opened the front door when we knocked. "Come on in," he said.

Inside it was wood floors, old-fashioned flowered wallpaper, and floor-to-ceiling bookcases on every wall full of those old vinyl records. I pulled some out while Eunice and Austin chatted. Mozart's collected violin sonatas. Shostakovich's Symphony No. 7. Rachmaninoff's Fourth Piano Concerto. Thousands and thousands of records, neatly lining every vertical surface in the front room, the hallway, and up the staircase to the second floor. Joab walked in the room wearing an apron that read "Kiss the Cook."

"You like Sibelius?" he asked, glancing at the record I happened to be holding.

"I'm not sure," I said. "I've never heard him."

"That's a good 'un," he said. "His violin concerto. Nothin' more beautiful than the sound of a violin in the hands of a master. Ain't that right, Austin?"

"Yes, sir," Austin said.

At that moment, Eli came down the stairs. He smiled when he saw me and we hugged, but he was more quiet and withdrawn than I was used to from him. Joab took Aunt Eunice to show her his garden and Austin went off to finish some chore or other. Eli and I were by ourselves in the entryway at the bottom of the stairs.

"So you're staying here?" I asked, surprised.

"Better'n spendin' nights alone back at my house."

I couldn't argue with that. I heard a meow and looked down to see a familiar white cat rubbing herself against my legs.

"Iloka!" I said. "You must plan on staying awhile if you brought her."

"Yep," Eli said.

"I'm amazed," I said. "I know you don't see eye to eye with Joab and Austin."

"Best option I got. Joab offered to let me stay 'til graduation. It's only a year." He picked Iloka up and stroked her under the chin. The cat cradled herself in his arms. "Problem is, I can hardly find my way to speak to either of 'em."

"Why is that?"

"Well, it ain't like I been too respectful towards Joab the last couple years, and here he takes me in like it's nothin'."

I thought of Eli's sarcasm at the hospital, and how it'd seemed to go over Joab's head. "He probably didn't even notice it," I said.

"Don't let him fool you, Dani," he said. "He might act backwoods, but he ain't dumb."

"You know, you could always apologize to him. That could help break the ice."

Iloka jumped out of Eli's arms and dashed off into the house. Eli looked away. "It ain't that easy."

"You could warm up by apologizing to me," I said.

Eli bit his lower lip. I didn't know if he was going to do it or not, and for a second I thought the suggestion had been one of those abrupt conversation-enders I tend to specialize in. But Eli stammered something, stopped, started again. "I...I'm sorry for what I done to you this summer, Dani. Everything that happened. I do mean that."

"Apology accepted," I said, smiling gently. I could sense how hard it had been for Eli. Time to change the subject. "So I guess you'll be going to church all the time now."

"Joab ain't said a word about it," Eli said, visibly relieved to talk about something else. "But that's what I mean about him bein' smarter than you think. If he'd said I had to go to church to stay here, I never would've done it. Now I'll probably end up going anyway."

Joab as a bumpkin country preacher? I could sense yet another preconception of mine falling away. More like a master psychologist. And classical music aficionado. And father of a music prodigy. I laughed. "Maybe he does have something figured out."

Our conversation was interrupted by Joab bellowing our names from outside the house. "I think he wants us to go to the garden," Eli said.

We went out the back door. Beyond a pen enclosed

in chicken wire and a muddy goat-chewed pasture we came to a square plot of land with neat rows of tomatoes and cucumbers interspersed by beds of marigolds. Aunt Eunice sat on a bench in the midst of well-tended rose bushes, bursting with blooms. Joab and Austin waited with violins and bows.

"I took the liberty of having Austin bring out your guitar," Joab said to Eli. "Hope you don't object."

"You want me to play somethin'?" Eli asked. Joab whispered in his ear and Eli nodded.

Aunt Eunice and I sat on the bench while the three guys positioned themselves. Joab counted off and they started in on the tune I recognized as *Arkansas Traveler*, though had you asked me two months before I would have said it was *Baby Bumble Bee*. After one time through the song with just the music, Joab put his fiddle down and started singing in a deep bass voice while Austin and Eli backed him up with their instruments.

> *Down in the mountains of Arkansas*
> *Visited the prettiest girl you ever saw*
> *She came from up North to live in our town*
> *And everyone was happy to have her come down*
> *She learned how we live and the music we play*
> *But now she can only stay here one more day*
> *And though her time here has nearly run*
> *We hope she won't forget us when it's done.*

They finished playing and Aunt Eunice and I clapped. I blushed from Joab's lyrics. They were silly, but I could tell they were heartfelt.

"Words're a little different from the last time I heard that song, Joab," Eli remarked.

"I adjusted 'em a bit for the occasion," Joab said. "Now y'all had best be sayin' your farewells because it's time the ladies got on their way."

Milling around saying good-bye for fifteen minutes is not my idea of a good time, so I gave all three guys a quick hug and made for Aunt Eunice's truck. Truth be told, I wanted to get out of there before the tears started. Aunt Eunice was kind enough to leave me be on the drive home while I had the faucets open.

The strangest thing was, despite everything he'd done, I was mainly crying because I would miss Eli. I wondered, was I like Emily, always ready to forgive my man and take him back, no matter what he did? But as I considered it, I realized I hadn't yet forgiven him. Maybe someday. But for the moment, I thought I understood him.

The next morning, there was a knock at my bedroom door early. Dad stuck his head in. "Someone here to see you, Dani," he said and closed the door.

Who the heck would be here at six in the morning? Aunt Eunice, probably. I didn't bother changing out of my nightgown and trudged out to the porch. When I opened the door, it was Eli, dressed like he always was, jeans, t-shirt, Razorbacks hat. Did he sleep in that outfit?

"You're up awfully early, aren't you?" I asked, blinking out the sleep in the early morning sunlight.

"I didn't want to miss you," he said. "And there's somethin' I got to say."

"I'm all ears." Birds twittered in the trees nearby.

"So I thought about what you said, about apologizin' to Joab and Austin and all. And so I did it."

"You did?" I asked.

"You say that like you don't believe me."

"No, I'm sorry. I do believe you," I said. "Good for you. What'd they say?"

"Nothin' much. Joab said he appreciated it. Austin only nodded. It ain't like him to talk if it ain't necessary."

"Yeah, I know," I said. "So it sounds like your accounts are all balanced now."

"Not yet," he said. "I do got one more apology to make. Down in Creekboro. But never mind that." He didn't say anything else, just stood staring at me expectantly.

"I could probably apologize too," I said. "For your face, I mean."

He ran his fingers along the raised marks on his cheek where I'd scratched him, pale and hairless against the pink of the rest of his skin. "Nah, don't apologize for that. It was my fault. You was only defendin' yourself."

"I'm afraid those scars will be permanent."

"I'll tell people I wrestled a *wasape*," he said.

I shook my head, not understanding.

"That's Osage for bear," he explained. He put a hand on the railing and turned to go. "Well, I reckon you got to pack and whatnot."

"Wait," I said. He looked back. "Come over here a second."

He stepped up to me and I tilted my head up. Our lips met. It didn't last long, but for a few moments, the whole summer distilled down to that one kiss. I shuddered as we parted. He pulled his hat down farther over his eyes. "Don't reckon we'll be seein' each other again," he said.

"Sure we will. I'll come back down with Mom for Eunice's court date."

"Well, I'll still be around," he said. "Let me know when you're back." He tipped his hat and grinned, turned, and went down the porch steps. "Be seein' you, *wasape*," he called. I watched as he drove off in his red pickup.

Seems I wasn't the only one who'd changed this summer. Eli apologizing for things he'd done wrong? Even a week before I wouldn't have believed it. And you know, it's fair to say his change, at least part of it, was due to me. Maybe I'd done some good in Adelaide during my time here, after all.

"Be seein' you," I said, and went back in the house.

The car was packed, the rental house closed up, the good-byes said. Dad, Ryan, and I stood by the Mustang. I don't know what we were waiting for. Just taking one last look around, I guess.

"Well guys, we'd better hit it," Dad said. "Who wants the front seat first?"

"Dani can have it," Ryan said nonchalantly.

"Really?" I asked.

"Yeah, go ahead."

"Thanks," I said, opening the door and sliding the seat forward so Ryan could climb in.

"You two sure you don't want to argue about it a little?" Dad said, his eyebrows raised.

"You know how she gets car sick when she sits in the back," Ryan said, putting on his seat belt.

"Huh," Dad said. He got in and pulled his door closed. He turned the key and the Mustang rolled forward off the lawn and into the street. He turned right at the farming equipment store and put the gas on. Only thirteen hours to Minneapolis.

I'd like to thank a number of people who have helped me in the writing and production of this book: John H. Matthews, Steve Moriarty, Pat Kallman, Barbara Osgood, Shea Megale, Joanna Pinto-Coelho, and all the members of the Writers of Chantilly who have helped me so much with your comments and encouragement over the years!

I hope you enjoyed reading *The Ballad of Dani and Eli!* Because Amazon reviews are one of the main drivers of book sales, please consider leaving a brief but honest review on this book's Amazon page.

Sign up for my mailing list and receive a free short story!
nicholasbruner.com/contact

Look for
Mother Ink
The first book of an epic fantasy trilogy by Nicholas Bruner coming in Fall 2021!